Summer's Coercion

The Season Series
Book 3

C M Stolworthy

 Boothpartnerspublishing
Words Shape Worlds

C M Stolworthy

SUMMER'S COERCION

THE SEASONS: BOOK 3

Copyright

Summer's Coercion
Book Three

 Formatted with Vellum

Thank you to my cover artist you are the best
Maria@ Ars Rönnei Media
I would like to thank my long suffering Husband who acts as IT
support.
Without you this would not happen.
And my son William who is now my publisher.
and Matthew who's help is amazing.

Chapter One

'Primrose, where are you?' Ash, the King of the Spring Elves, marched along the corridor of the manor house. He smiled as he pushed the door to her bedchamber open.

'You could have knocked.' Primrose spun around. A frown marring her brow. Seeing his faltering step, she smiled before rushing into his arms, feeling his arms wrap around her.

'Wow, I can get my arms all the way around now,' Ash chuckled. 'Can I see her?' Ash untangled himself from Primrose.

'Um, Ash, about that... I need to explain,' Primrose stuttered, trying to put her body between him and the cradle.

'Primrose, you know I must see her. The Elder Council will want to know.' Brushing his black hair back, he peered into the cradle, his eyes opening wide with shock as he sucked in a gulp of air. 'Primrose, there are two,' Ash whispered.

'Yes, it would seem so. Oh, Ash, what do we do?' Primrose looked at him with tears in her eyes. 'What will the Elder Council do?'

'I... I don't know,' Ash frowned as he looked at the twin girls.

'Do we have to tell them? You know, we could just not say,' she pleaded.

'We can't have two children of nature. We can't have two Mother Natures,' Ash explained as he gazed mesmerised by the sleeping babies. His mind was in turmoil. He needed to go to the Elder Council. Hyperion was the wisest of them all, and he would have a solution.

'I know,' she bit her lip. 'Do we have to tell them there are two though? They don't really need to know do they? Couldn't we... just hide one?'

'We need to tell the Elder Council everything, we can't conceal this. It is unprecedented. Only they can decide.' Ash gathered her into his arms.

Ash stepped out of the tree, its glowing dissipating as he stepped away. He walked with a sombre gait through the glade to the log cabin that stood just at the edge of the clearing. This he knew would be where he would find his younger brother and King of the Autumn Elves and his sister, Queen of the Spring Elves. He walked up to the cabin and went around the side where he could hear wood being chopped.

Laran stood, his shirt hanging from a nearby tree, as he chopped logs and threw them into a pile, the late afternoon sun highlighting his dark auburn hair as his honey toned skin glistened with sweat from his exertions. He looked up, startled, his axe in mid-air when Ash appeared.

'Ash, great to see you.' Laran put his axe down. Picking up an old rag, he wiped the sweat from his face and body. 'What can I do for you?' Laran enquired, filling a basket with freshly split logs.

'You, erm ... finished?' Ash indicated the basket.

'Yeah, just wanted enough for tonight,' Laran answered as Ash tossed him his shirt.

'Is Anahuit about?'

'Oh yes, she is inside cooking dinner. Are you staying? Say you will,' Laran pleaded.

'Yes, I will stay,' Ash answered as he walked round to the cabin door. He pushed the door to the cabin open to find Anahuit inside dressed in traditional costume for the period. Her black hair was in a plait over her shoulder. Ash shrugged and smiled.

'Ash, what news?' She asked, watching Ash's face seeing his expression change to sadness. As his smile faded, his mouth became a thin line.

'The baby, is it alright?' Anahuit asked.

'Yes, it's fine,' Ash managed.

'Primrose, she is alright?'

'Yes... It´s twins, Ana. I don't know what to do.'

'Twins, Ash, really, I'm not falling for that, you idiot. Be serious.'

'I am being serious. She had twins.'

'Twins? How can that be?' Laran demanded from the door of the cabin, through which he had just entered. 'There can only be one Child of Nature at any one time. Those were the laws that were laid down in the beginning,' he demanded. He leaned his axe against the wall.

'I'm not sure. It was so long ago, I don't really remember,' Anahuit replied with a look of confusion.

'Well Ash, you've got an excellent memory. You must remember what we need to do,' Laran asked.

'Well, I usually have an excellent memory when I'm not

drunk,' he replied with a chuckle.

'Surely you weren't...' Laran asked with a mixture of shock and disgust.

'At the beginning, oh yes, completely trashed. To be fair, it is all a bit of a drunken blur before 4,000 BC. Those Romans knew how to throw a party,' he shrugged, a sheepish smile on his face.

'I actually cannot believe you right now,' Anahuit scolded him.

'What? You were no better yourself?'

'Meh, true,' she responded.

'Enough. Andarta will remember and Hyperion will know what to do. We need to call a gathering,' Laran ordered.

'You're right,' Anahuit agreed.

'Alright, I'll arrange it; you two stay here and keep on with your weird cabin in the woods thing you've got going on,' Ash said as he walked towards the cabin door.

'Anyway, I'll be off now. You two have fun,' Ash said as he opened the cabin door and strode off into the early evening sun.

Ash stepped out of the tree in front of a Scottish medieval castle, striding across the lawn and banged on the oak front door to be greeted by Solstice, Queen of the Winter Elves. Dressed in a long velvet gown, her silver hair tied up in an intricate bun.

'Solstice, you look... amazing,' Ash stuttered. What the hell was going on? He was shaking his head as Solstice ushered him into the castle.

'Oh, this old thing? Had it lying around since last century.

Taranis isn't adapting to the industrial revolution thing too well, bless him,'

'Well, he seemed to fit into the whole feudal lord role rather well,' Ash managed.

'Have you brought news?' Solstice asked eagerly.

'Yes, I need to see Taranis,' Ash answered, striding purposefully along the corridor toward the throne room.

Taranis, the King of the Winter, elves was languishing in his large oaken throne. Two long tables ran the length of the room, fully laden with gleaming silver cutlery, plates, and goblets. The entire room was bustling with servants and attendants preparing for another of Taranis's legendary feasts.

'Ash, so good to see you. Where have you been for the last hundred years, brother?' Taranis bellowed, noticing Ash striding towards him amidst the servant's hustle and bustle.

'Ah, you know me. I like to get around,' Ash replied with a grin.

'Still trying to outrun all those fair maidens you keep bedding and their angry mothers?' Taranis' violet eyes twinkled with mischief.

'Something like that,' Ash chuckled, 'but what about you? It seems married life suits you?'

'Indeed. Can you believe Solstice finally got me to settle down? I'm not even allowed to go pillaging across the border anymore,' Taranis complained, a sullen look on his face.

'Well, no, of course not. It's 1732, the English and the Scottish aren't really into that anymore.'

'I know, it's a matter of principle. Hell, I miss the Vikings,' he sighed, a lost look in his eye.

'Oh, get over yourself. Anyway, that's not the reason I came. We have a problem and the entire council's opinion will be needed before we decide what to do.'

'My dear chap, your appearance is fortuitous as tomorrow.

All the sixteen and their entourages are arriving for our annual meeting,' Taranis beamed, feeling rather pleased with himself.

'Well, that is marvellous! We need to assemble the Elder Council as well.' Ash closed his eyes briefly and reached out to Anahuit through their telepathic link. Smiling as he felt her nudge, he relayed the message, knowing that Anahuit would tell Laran to contact Andarta, Queen of the Autumn Elves. Anahuit replied that Andarta was with Alectrona, Queen of the Summer Elves, and would pass the message on.

'Why? What has happened? I heard our dear Mother Nature, Primrose, had gone into labour. Has she passed during childbirth?' Taranis sat up straight, a worried frown etched into his brow.

'No. She is fine, and so is the baby. There has been another complication.'

'You have me well and truly intrigued. If I recall correctly, you never used to be so evasive. Well, everyone will arrive soon, so we'll soon sort this out.' Taranis replied with a cheerful voice as he climbed to his feet. 'In the meantime, come see my new horse

'Ash, I don't like this. What do you think they will do?' Primrose jiggled the baby girls in her arms, her entire posture agitated. Her gaze scrutinised the front facade of the castle, finally resting on the imposing oak doors. As the babies fussed, sensing their mother's agitation, Ash reached over and placed a calming hand on her arm, and with a smile, took one baby expertly, putting it to his shoulder and rubbing her back in a soothing motion.

'I don't know, nothing like this has ever happened before,' Ash replied, trying to keep his voice light so as not to alarm Primrose further. 'You are Mother Nature, let's not forget that.' his smile was to reassure, but he wasn't sure it convinced anyone.

As Ash led Primrose through the oak doors and toward the banqueting hall, he could already hear voices. Everyone else had already arrived. A door opened and a young woman emerged. Her black hair and blue eyes identified her as a spring elf. She hurried up to them, throwing her arms around Primrose and the baby in a hug.

'Narcissus, I am so glad you are here,' Primrose said, managing a weak smile.

'Of course, I'm here. I'm your Guardian Elf and that now extends to these two.' She took the baby from Ash's arms. 'Right, let's do this,' she turned on her heel and pushed open the large oak front doors into the entrance hall. Primrose and Ash followed behind.

The room fell silent as all eyes turned towards Primrose. Ash noticed that the two tables from the day before had increased to four. They had placed one long table sideways in front of the raised platform that Taranis' throne sat upon.

The entire Elder Council was seated at the table with Hyperion, King of the Summer Elves, the oldest and wisest of the eight immortals of the seasons in the middle, facing the door. He dutifully rose to his feet as he saw Primrose approaching, his smile revealing his perfect white teeth. His gleaming gold hair framed his handsome face.

Primrose took in Hyperion's immaculate outfit. A gold waistcoat beneath a bright crimson jacket. She did not smile back and walked silently between the four tables where each of the season houses sat. She stood directly in front of Hyperion and surveyed everyone at the table; the baby clasped in her arms. Alectrona, as Queen of Summer, was seated to Hyperion's right, with Taranis to his left. Next to him was Solstice, Anahuit next to her, and then an empty seat for Ash at the end. To the right of Alectrona were Laran and Andarta.

'Mother Nature, it's good to see you. I'm so glad to hear that the birth went without complications. And twins, no less,' Alectrona pushed to her feet, a welcoming smile on her lips as she brushed down her skirt that matched Hyperion's waist coat in colour and style.

'Thank you, Alectrona. If only the circumstances were a little different,' Primrose replied.

'Indeed. Since the beginning, there has never been an instance wherein two Children of Nature were born at the same time and as such, the Council is unsure how to proceed,' Hyperion said, having taken his seat once more. Meanwhile, Ash walked around the table and took his seat next to Anahuit.

'The ramifications of this are far-reaching and difficult to discern. However, I am of the opinion that two Children of Nature together are far too dangerous a state of affairs to be acceptable. At the very least, we must separate the infants,' Hyperion said before casting a look down the table to see what any of the others thought.

'Please, Hyperion, we don't even know if both of the children will be gifted or not. It may be that one of them is the true Child of Nature and the other is normal,' Ash reasoned.

'Or maybe they are both fully powered, in which case think of what they could achieve. If we took care of them and if they worked together, they could usher in a new age of peace and harmony,' Alectrona said, a strange look in her eye.

'They could be turned against us. It would be difficult for the Council of Elders to remove even one Mother Nature once they are fully powered. If they used two of them against us, or each other, we wouldn't stand a chance,' Taranis replied.

'I'm of a mind with Taranis on this one, my love; if they fell into the wrong hands, the results could be dire for elves and humans. They could raise mountains and drown continents. We must separate them,' Hyperion said.

'Separated is not enough. The danger would not have passed. They could still find one of them, still be turned. We must kill one to return balance. This abomination cannot persist,' Taranis argued.

'That can't be!' Andarta demanded, while Primrose screamed and began sobbing.

'Hyperion, talk sense into him. We can't just kill an infant for crimes it may not even commit,' Anahuit demanded.

'I'm afraid I cannot. This is unheard of, and I believe Taranis is right. The risks are too great. Either we remove the threat now or it may be too late,' Hyperion announced, his voice sage and calm.

'You can't seriously be advocating the killing of a child,' Solstice complained.

'That's exactly what I'm suggesting. I'm afraid I just cannot see a better solution,' Hyperion reasoned.

'Surely any solution that doesn't involve infanticide?' Andarta suggested.

'Thank you, Andarta, but unless you have a solution to offer us, comments such as that are not productive,' Alectrona chided.

'You can't kill one of my babies. I will not allow it,' Primrose sobbed.

'I am sorry, Mother Nature, but I agree with Hyperion and Taranis - there is no other way,' Alectrona said, before taking a sip from a silver goblet in front of her.

'What about you, Laran? You've said nothing this entire time. What would you suggest?' Ash demanded as he leaned forward to look all the way along the table to where Laran was sitting silently.

'The dark elves have recently become more motivated and better coordinated than ever before. If they kidnapped one of the Children of Nature and somehow alienated them against us, the resulting damage they could cause would be unparalleled.'

'So, you agree? We must kill one infant?' Hyperion asked.

Laran replied after a brief pause.

'Yes,'

'No! You can't do this! It's just a baby, it has done nothing wrong!' Primrose shouted through her tears, as the sky darkened outside, and rain patted against the window.

Sensing the change in atmospheric pressure, Hyperion calmly rose to his feet. 'Primrose, please remain calm. Let's not do anything that any of us will regret.'

'What? Like murder an innocent baby?' Primrose argued, thunder cracking outside.

'We have no other choice; it must be done.'

'You say that Hyperion, but talking about killing an infant and actually murdering one are two entirely different things. Are you sure any of us here could really do the deed?' Andarta asked sceptically.

'If it is what we must do, I will dispose of the infant,' Laran announced gravely.

'It is settled then,' Hyperion concluded.

'No, it is not. Hyperion, you gave the order, therefore it is only fitting that you carry out the deed, is it not?' Anahuit asked calmly.

'I agree. If it must be done, as it was your idea, you should be the one to do it, Hyperion,' Solstice said.

Hyperion looked troubled by this. But after a moment's hesitation, he appeared to find his resolve and spoke up. 'So be it. If it's what we must do, I shall make it so,' Hyperion announced, accompanied by another wave of sobbing from Primrose.

'In that case, if there is nothing more to discuss, then this meeting is adjourned. Primrose, I will give you some time to say your goodbyes to the child before I take it,' Hyperion said, his face set with grim resolve.

The other Elders stood to leave, Anahuit rushing to Primrose's side and putting her arms around her before ushering her from the hall, her sobbing echoing through the chamber for a while after they left.

Slowly, the other Elders and Lords filtered from the hall. Feeling thoroughly miserable and his appetite having completely deserted him, Ash stood to leave the room. He strode around the end table and between the four tables set out for the Lords and into the lobby.

'Ash! Ash! Wait!' Alectrona shouted as she followed him out of the hallway.

'What is it, Alectrona? Shouldn't you be busy sharpening an axe for Hyperion or something?' Ash asked bitterly.

'Oh, come on Ash, we both saw the look on Hyperion's face when Anahuit and Solstice made him do it. If it was down to Laran, the child would already be dead,' Alectrona argued as she led him down a side corridor and into a deserted drawing room. Shelves filled with books lined the walls as a warming fire crackled in the hearth.

'So, what's your point?' Ash asked.

'My point is, despite the number of infants that he has condemned to death over the years, he's feeling a little nervous. He doesn't have what it takes. If someone slightly more manly were to volunteer, I expect he wouldn't hesitate to delegate the task,' Alectrona said in a deep, husky voice.

Ash could feel her hand on his chest as he stared into her seductive, caramel brown eyes. 'Are you saying that I should do it? I don't even think that I agree with his decision in the first place,' Ash grumbled. He thought he saw a frown flash across her face, but it was difficult to tell in the half-light from the fire.

'I'm saying that you can put yourself forward to do it. Then the decision about what happens to the infant is yours,' she whispered in his ear. Ash could feel her warm breath on his neck and took a slight step backward.

'Alright. I'll do it. But this stays between us,' He decided, trying to sound assertive and retake control of the conversation. He wasn't particularly used to being on the receiving end of a charm offensive.

'Our little secret, darling,' Alectrona smiled seductively over her shoulder as she left the room.

Ash strode purposefully from the room not long after her, turning left towards the entrance hall where Alectrona had gone right. He made his way past the main staircase along another corridor. He knew that at this hour, Hyperion, Taranis and possibly Laran would be drinking in the billiards room.

The sound of Taranis' laughter greeted him as he peered around the door into the room. Hyperion, Laran, and Taranis were sat huddled in the corner, drinking and smoking cigars.

'Ash, old boy, why don't you come join us?' Taranis asked jovially.

'Well, I'd love to, old chap. But first, Hyperion, if you've got a minute, can I have a word, please?'

'How mysterious,' Hyperion said as he rose to his feet. 'Of course, just a moment, gents.' Hyperion stood, crossed the room, and followed Ash into the hall.

'So, what's this about Ash?' Hyperion asked.

'It's about the child.'

'Ah, yes, horrible business,' Hyperion responded.

'I was just thinking it might be better for Primrose if I did the deed. We always were close. I just thought that she might trust me more...to...to be more...erm...humane. If you catch my meaning?' He broke eye contact to appear more nervous.

'Well, when you put it like that, it makes more sense if you handle it. In fact, you'd be doing me a favour, old boy. I wasn't really looking forward to it if I'm honest. Infanticide...is, well, it's quite distasteful if I must say. Especially in these civilised times,' Hyperion replied.

'Well, there we have it then. I think I'll go now and get it over with,' Ash said with a terse smile, turning on his heel and striding away.

'Ash, please no,' Primrose begged him as he walked up to her.

'I'm sorry, Primrose, but it must be done. Don't worry, I promise it will be quick and painless,' Ash said as he took the baby, his face set in stone.

'No...,' Primrose whimpered. Narcissus rushed to her side with the other baby, placing her arm around Primrose. Anahuit stood watching Ash, a pensive frown marring her features as she tried to work out why Ash would volunteer to do such a horrible thing.

He held the small baby against his chest and walked determinedly away from Primrose, his electric blue eyes all the while fixed on the great oak doors before him, Primrose's renewed wailing ringing in his ears.

'Ash, wait!' Anahuit ran, catching up and slipping into step with him, pushing the doors open as he strode across the lawn where a large ancient scots pine stood.

'Shouldn't you be in there with Laran?' Ash glanced at her as he reached the tree, the baby mewling in his arms.

'Ash, please you can't, it's a baby for pity's sake,' she reached out her hand and placed it on his arm, preventing him from touching the bark, therefore stalling his departure so she could have her say.

'I'd have thought that you at least know me well enough to realise that I have absolutely no intention of killing this baby,' he answered, his voice full of anger and his mouth set in a hard line as he glared at her through narrowed eyes.

'Oh, thank goodness. But if you aren't going to kill it, what will you do with it?' Anahuit sighed with relief clear in her voice as she gazed at him.

'I'm not sure... I was thinking of returning it to Primrose later when the time is right,' he confessed.

Anahuit scowled. 'That would never work. Hyperion would find out in a flash. If he learns you disobeyed him, he'll make us suffer for it.' Anahuit looked around and then back at him. 'We should hide her, keep her safe. There must be a reason that two Children of Nature were born. We just don't understand what it is yet.'

'Where do you propose we hide it, exactly?' Ash asked, relaxing slightly.

'Far away from the Elder Council. We can raise her as our own and keep her line safe until the time comes. When the reason we have her becomes clear.'

Ash gazed at her. She was almost his mirror image, so perfectly matched he sometimes knew what she was thinking before she thought about it. He knew she was right. But this was so dangerous. If they were found out, there was no telling what would happen.

'I know a place. But aren't you supposed to be with Laran?

You two looked pretty happy together the other day, with the whole cabin in the woods thing you've got going on.'

'After what he said in there?' Anahuit shook her head. 'He would have killed that baby in a heartbeat and not lost a wink of sleep over it. I'm over him.'

'Isn't he going to miss you?' Ash asked, still not completely convinced.

'Don't you worry about him, I can take care of him without too much trouble,' Anahuit smiled, kissing him on the cheek before linking her arm with his as he reached out and touched the tree.

Alectrona stood silently in one of the first-floor corridors. Hyperion, Laran, and Taranis were still in the entrance hall eating, drinking, and swapping stories of their misadventures. Andarta and Solstice were still there too. Alectrona had excused herself on the pretence of urgent business to attend to and slipped away. She had watched as Ash and Anahuit stood and discussed something by a tree at the edge of the forest that surrounded the castle. Ash had still been holding the baby and after a short period, Anahuit had leaned in and kissed him before the pair of them vanished in a flash of golden light. Alectrona couldn't have heard what they had been talking about, but it was easy to guess. Ash had done exactly what she had wanted him to. Alectrona had no idea what use another Nature Child would have, but she was certain it would be more useful to her alive than dead.

Chapter Two

The last lesson of the day seemed to Willow to drag on forever. She had her head resting on one of her hands as she listened to the droning voice of her chemistry teacher. Her long mahogany hair falling like a curtain around her face, obscuring it from view. All day, a niggling headache had been building. Although hurting wasn't the right word, it was more like buzzing. Sometimes she could hear voices, as if a radio had been left on in her head and she couldn't switch it off.

Jacen nudged her as the bell went, indicating the end of another very dull day. He had noticed that Willow had been unusually quiet all day, and now he was looking at her closely.

'Come on, Willow, let's get the bus,' Jacen nudged Willow again. Gently, he brushed her hair to one side, his hazel eyes creased with concern.

Willow opened her eyes and shoved her books into her schoolbag, her gaze drifting over his features, seeing the crease of his brow as be brushed his unruly, dirty blond hair from his eyes that crinkled with concern. That, in her opinion, just made him look adorable. She followed him outside.

'Willow, Willow,' Jane ran up, bending over, getting her breath back.

'Hi Jane,' Willow smiled at her friend, watching as she flicked her brown hair away from her face. Her blue eyes landed on Jacen, causing heat to colour her cheeks.

'Jake wants to know if you're going to his party on Saturday. He's been pestering me all day to ask you. I'm sure he has a crush on you,' Jane grinned as she saw Jacen scowling.

'Oh... um, I'm not sure.' Willow looked at Jacen.

'Yeah, tell him we will be there,' said Jacen, slightly annoyed at being put on the spot. He was running his hand through his hair, making it stick up at odd angles. For a moment Jane just stared at him unblinking, drinking him in.

'Oh great, see you there. Must go, my mum's waiting.' Jane turned, dragging her gaze away from Jacen and running over to a large smart looking car parked outside the school gates. Jacen slipped his hand into Willow's as they walked to the bus stop, just so everyone would know she was with him.

'Are you alright, Willow?'

'Um yes, just tired and headachy, that's all,' Willow replied as they found seats together.

'What are you doing during the holidays?' Asked Jacen. Tomorrow was their last day of term, and they had an entire week off stretching before them.

'Nothing, as far as I know,' Willow replied, resting her head on his shoulder, and closing her eyes. The voices had started in her head again, all talking at once. She felt like she was standing in a crowded room. Willow felt Jacen put his arm round her. He was, without doubt, the best friend in the world. She thought about the kiss and then she thought about the boy at the castle and felt guilty. She should forget about him. William was right. Gail was way out of her league. But she still felt apprehensive about forming a proper relationship with Jacen. What if they broke up and he never spoke to her ever again? Selfish as it may be, she knew she couldn't risk that. But what if they were together? She sighed. Why did everything have to be so difficult where boys were concerned?

'Well, we just need to get through tomorrow and then the week is our own,' Jacen grinned, his fingers twinning with hers. Guiding her onto the bus, to the seat he preferred.

'Hey Willow, going to kill your brother again this holiday?' came a voice from the back of the bus. Willow sighed and opened her eyes. It was those damn twins and their little gang. They always sat at the back of the bus. Sometimes Willow had a really hard time remembering that Jacen was related to them.

Willow turned around and smiled sweetly. 'Only if you kiss him again and he begs me to end his life,' Willow replied. Laughter followed this from all around the bus. The twins glared furiously at her; their faces flushed with embarrassment.

The bus arrived at Willow's stop and Jacen got off the bus too, walking with her. As they walked down the drive towards the house, Heli appeared. Heli was Willow's guardian elf and came from the house of summer. Her full name was Helianthus, or sunflower.

'Hi Heli,' Jacen said, putting his hand in his pocket and producing a small chocolate bar, which he then offered to Heli. Heli grinned and happily accepted it before skipping off down the drive. Her bright yellow hair fluttered in the breeze as she skipped.

Jacen watched Heli with a smile. His relationship with Heli was far more complex than his relationship with Willow. Although Heli looked eight most of the time, she was the same age as him and he knew he loved her and would protect her; except sometimes he wasn't sure about his feelings toward her. It certainly wasn't the same sort of love he felt for his sisters, but not the same feelings he felt for Willow. Jacen reached for Willow's hand, glad when she didn't pull away.

Willow glanced at Jacen, wondering if he would kiss her again. 'You know when you proclaimed that having an elf was cooler than having a dog that afternoon when we were five, I thought Heli would never talk to you again.'

Jacen laughed 'I remember she sulked for ages. It was a good thing I had that chocolate in my pocket,' he chuckled.

'Yes, well, I'm not sure I approve of the chocolate bribery-based friendship you two have, especially when she changes her appearance to look like a teenage girl,' Willow grumbled.

'Are you jealous?' Jacen chuckled.

'You know you will rot her teeth with all that chocolate,' remarked Willow.

'Do an elf's teeth rot?' Inquired Jacen. Willow shrugged, not really knowing the answer. Heli and the other guardian elves could change her appearance at will. Now, she looked like an eight-year-old girl. The guardian elves seemed to like this look, as it helped them blend in better. Humans were strange in that they paid very little attention to certain age groups.

The house was empty, as usual. Willow and Jacen made a drink and found the latest cake her mum had baked - a lemon drizzle. Willow sat at the kitchen table. She didn't want to go into the other room and watch television like they normally did. She just wanted to sit in silence with her eyes closed. Jacen noticed this and after eating his piece of lemon drizzle cake, made his excuses to go home.

'I am sorry, Jacen. Will I see you Saturday before the party?' Willow asked, getting up as Jacen walked to the door.

'Yeah, I can come over late morning if you like. I've got to help Dad on the farm. I said I would milk the cows for him so he could take Mum out on Friday night. Some do at the pub, I think.'

He smiled and without thinking, leaned in and kissed her. Willow closed her eyes, enjoying the feeling, her body pressed against his, his hands on her waist. She opened her mouth. He made a funny growl from his throat and ran his hands up her back. Eventually, he pulled away and, smiling shyly, he quietly closed the door behind him and headed down the lane back to his house.

Willow tidied up their plates and cups and then went upstairs to change out of her school uniform. She thought about the kiss with Jacen; it had been nice. Although she still couldn't decide what their relationship was as they went out together all the time before he had kissed her, but was it considered dating now with the kissing? Did he think she was his girlfriend? Willow sighed. She was tempted to lie on her bed but decided to go and find her older brother and dad. Willow picked up her phone. To her amazement, she noticed a text from a number she wasn't familiar with.

17.25, Gail
Hey, how r u? your mum gave me your number hope u don't mind.

Willow gave a small squeal of delight once she realised who it was from. Sometimes her mum was the best. Sitting on her bed, she tried several times to compose a reply.

17.26, Willow
No, don't mind, how r u? is your neck better.

. . .

17.27, Gail

Yeah, thks. I am fine. wot u doing.

17.27, Willow

Nothing just got in.

17.28, Gail

Would u like to go out on sat?? cinema or something???
As I am in London.

Oh my goodness ran through her head several times. He was asking her on a date. Heli sauntered in, having heard Willows squeal. Without saying a word, Willow held her phone out to Heli, who then squealed as well.

'I thought you were going to Jake's party with Jacen Saturday?'

'Oh yeah, forgot about that,' Willow slumped with disappointment.

'You could cancel,' Heli raised a brow.

'I can't do that,'

'Well, what about Sunday?'

'Yes!' Willow grabbed Heli in a spine crushing hug.

17.28, Willow

Sorry going out with Jacen to Jakes party.

17.29, Gail

Oh!!! Is he your boyfriend??

. . .

17.29, Willow
> *No silly*
> *I'm free on Sunday. I can meet up with you then.*

17.30, Gail
> *Great, I will txt a time later* 😊

Grabbing Heli, both girls danced about the room before flopping onto the bed.

'How did he get your number?'

'Mum gave it to him,'

'Sometimes Lilly is amazing,' Heli giggled.

'Are you going to tell Jacen?'

'Should I?'

'I don't know,'

'Maybe wait to see how this pans out. I might not like him, you know, in a non-life-threatening setting,'

'Yeah, right,' Heli drawled while rolling her eyes.

Willow wandered down the path towards the greenhouses, a big grin on her face.

They were huge Victorian glass houses and David, her dad, had spent years lovingly restoring them. David and William, Willows older brother, spent a lot of time down here. They were very close and sometimes, when Willow came down here, she felt like the odd one out. There had even been occasions when she had felt a little jealous of William.

The voices in Willow's head had started again. She felt cold. They were the same as the ones during the summer when she had been in the meadow with Jacen. Back then, she couldn't control them, and they had overwhelmed her. Now she had better control, but still not enough to block them out completely. She rubbed her temples tiredly. Willow walked past the third greenhouse and stopped. Something was in there, and it was calling out her name. Willow turned and was about to go in when William appeared.

'Willow, what are you doing down here?' He signed, smiling with pleasure at seeing his sister.

'Oh. I was looking for you and Dad. What's in there?' Willow asked, motioning towards the greenhouse with her head. 'I thought I heard a voice.'

'Just the usual, as far as I know. What sort of voice?' William asked, concerned. 'Please, no more drama. I have a date with Suzy tonight,' William realised too late that he had signed that last bit by mistake. He dropped his hand, hoping Willow hadn't noticed. She narrowed her eyes and fixed her gaze on him, seeing him squirm. She noticed.

'Spill,' she demanded, seeing the blush stain his cheeks.

'What? It's nothing, taking her to the pub, that's all. So, this voice, what did it sound like?' he repeated, trying to steer her attention away from him.

'Um, a very seductive, female voice.' Willow replied, making a mental note to grill him in the morning.

'That's weird, I can't hear anything.'

'You're deaf, you idiot,' Willow looked at William and they both burst out laughing.

'Dad's down in the office in the first greenhouse. Come on, I can show you, I'm going that way.' William linked his arm with Willow's. She looked awfully pale.

'Are you alright, Willow?'

'Yeah, tired, that's all,' replied Willow as they stepped into the first greenhouse. She adored her big brother and was very protective of him. Until recently, the village girls hadn't paid him any attention. But since last year, he had changed from the bumbling deaf kid. With his startling green eyes and messy curly auburn hair. He had lost his puppy fat, gaining muscle definition from working in the garden centre with their dad. Willow could see the attraction. Heli was right, William had got buff.

As Willow walked past the row of plants, they all seemed to grow a bit and turn in her direction, as if they wanted her attention.

'Hi, Dad,' said Willow as she entered the office to find David sitting looking at a picture of some sort of beetle on his computer screen. He turned, smiling, his hair as messy as Williams.

'Hi sweetheart, what brings you down here? Where's Jacen?' David replied.

'He's gone home,' Willow said, absentmindedly stroking the soft furry petal of velvet red Gloxinia, which immediately burst into flower.

'Dad, what's in Greenhouse Three?' She asked, trying to sound casual.

'Oh, just a plant I brought home from work. Someone was trying to smuggle it into the country. I need to figure out what it is so we can send it back to wherever it came from. Why?' David worked for the Food and Environmental Research agency, or FERA, as a botanist. It was the same government organisation as Willow's mum.

'Can I see it?' Asked Willow

'Yes, of course you can. But it's not that interesting, is it, William?' Replied David with a slightly puzzled expression, wondering why Willow was suddenly so interested in his work.

'No, not really,' said William, reaching for the key to Greenhouse Three. Willow followed David and William up the path. As they got nearer the greenhouse, the voice started in Willow's head.

'*Can you hear that, William?*' She asked. As both little elves were with them, the telepathic link was open. William frowned and concentrated, and then nodded.

'What is that, Willow?' He asked, looking at her.

'I'm not sure, but it's coming from in there.' David had stopped and was unlocking the door. Willow instinctively took hold of William's hand as they stepped inside. The voice in Willow's head grew so loud that even William covered his ears. The voice was soft but still blocked out all other sounds as it saturated his brain, shutting his link to Willow and the elves, begging him to touch it.

'Willow, we should go,' he shouted, causing David to jump.

'William, why are you shouting?' David demanded crossly.

'Dad, I have this voice in my head. Can't you hear it?'

'No, William, I can't. What does it say?' David pulled William around so he could see his face.

'It wants me, it wants to touch me, it wants me to set it free.'

The greenhouse was dark and musty inside. The light from the door falling upon what was, in Willow's opinion, the most beautiful plant she had ever seen. It covered the entire greenhouse in thick tendrils that now and then sprouted large trumpet shaped, blood-red flowers that gave off a thick pungent aroma.

Willow felt her arms growing heavy and her vision fogging as she breathed in the plant's narcotic scent. It was so... beautiful; she had to touch it. She stepped forward and reached out to its dark green tendrils, which, sensing her presence, moved slowly towards her to ensnare her in their embrace.

'It wasn't this big when I put it in here the other day,' David said to the children, his comments falling on deaf ears as the plants' mesmerising beauty enchanted them.

'Willow, what are you doing?' He asked. 'Stop it. That might be poisonous.' Moving quickly, he grabbed Willow's arms to pull her back. She struggled against him. He got his arms around her waist and was slowing her down when she lashed out with her elbow, smacking him squarely in the face.

'I must touch it,' she said. 'It wants me to. It needs me,' Willow said, her voice emotionless.

'William, help me!' David cried, as he picked himself up off the floor.

William ignored him and started walking towards the plant. 'So pretty,' he mumbled, as he reached out to it.

Heli immediately cut off the telepathic link between the siblings, and William could feel the fog slowly lifting from his mind. Heli gave him a kick in the shin to focus his attention.

'Ow! What was that for?' He cried, glaring at Heli.

'Help David!' She commanded. Between father and son, they took hold of Willow's arms and dragged her from the greenhouse. Willow struggled desperately and banged her head hard on the doorframe as they forced her through. She momentarily lost her senses, the plant losing its hold over her.

William carefully laid her down on the grass in front of the greenhouse while David locked the door.

'Willow, what was that?' William asked, noticing his hands were shaking.

'It needs my help,' replied Willow, trying to get up. 'I.... don't know. I have had these voices in my head all day calling me, asking for my help and I couldn't shut them out like I normally can. I'm scared, William. I want Mum.'

'It's all right, Willow. Mum will probably be home from work soon. In the meantime, I suggest you all stay away from that greenhouse, understand?' David ordered them, deeply concerned that Willow seemed to have had some sort of episode induced by that strange plant. And how could it have been talking to them?

'You don't need to tell us twice, Dad.' William signed before wrapping an arm around his sister.

Chapter Three

Willow sat in English class next to Jacen, feeling... off.

Not ill, exactly. Just wrong. Like something had slipped half a step out of place and hadn't bothered to come back again.

For the fifth time in as many minutes, she checked her phone, willing the lesson to end. They were studying *Lord of the Flies*, which, in Willow's opinion, was a small miracle in how spectacularly boring it managed to make a nuclear apocalypse. She'd never understood how you could strand children on an island and not get at least one explosion out of it.

Their teacher certainly wasn't helping. Miss Harringdon stood at the front of the room, droning on about literary techniques and the protagonist's journey of self-discovery, as though that was the interesting part. From Willow's perspective, the main character was a bit of a pansy, Piggy was irritating, and the only journey worth mentioning involved weapons, fire, and considerably more chaos.

She shifted in her seat. The classroom felt cold. Not properly cold — just enough that she couldn't get comfortable, no matter how she tucked her arms in or pulled her jumper tighter.

She slipped her phone into her lap and texted Gail.

14:45, Willow:

So bored and feel odd

14:45, Gail:

What u doing? I'm bored 2. In some dull meeting. How do you mean odd? 😕

Willow frowned at the screen, trying to work out how to explain something she didn't understand herself. Her head buzzed faintly, like a radio tuned just off station. Not voices — not yet — but pressure. Crowded. Expectant.

Cold slid down her spine, sharp enough to make her gasp.

Something icy brushed her cheek.

She blinked and looked up.

A single snowflake drifted lazily down from the ceiling and landed squarely on Jacen's nose.

He went cross-eyed, trying to look at it, then glanced at the window. Bright sunshine. Blue sky. Not a cloud in sight. All the windows were firmly shut.

'Er... Willow,' he said slowly, turning back to her, 'I think we need to go.'

More snowflakes appeared. At first just a few, then more, forming out of nothing, settling on desks and exercise books. Breath fogged in the air.

For a heartbeat, no one moved.

Thirty children stared as snow gathered where it had no right to be.

Miss Harringdon opened her mouth.

A snowball smacked into the side of her head.

The room exploded.

Someone whooped. Someone else laughed. Within seconds, snowballs were flying from every direction. Chairs scraped back, pupils ducked and shrieked, and Miss Harringdon vanished into the supply cupboard with a yelp.

'Jacen, how do I make it stop?' Willow whispered, panic clawing up her throat. The buzzing in her head was louder now, layered and relentless.

Jacen didn't answer. He grabbed her hand and hauled her to her feet, ducking a snowball as it whizzed past his ear.

'Come on!'

They bolted for the door, snow exploding against the walls around them. The corridor beyond was no better. Every classroom they passed was caught in its own miniature blizzard. Teachers shouted in confusion. Students cheered like it was the best day of their lives.

Willow stumbled, her legs numb, the cold inside her deepening until it felt lodged in her bones.

They burst through the double doors into the playground.

'Don't worry, we'll get out of—' Jacen yelped and snatched his hand away. 'Willow! Your hand's freezing!'

'I'm sorry!' Her voice shook. 'I don't know what's happening.'

'I know. It's okay. Just—just keep moving.'

They ran. Past the school gates, down two streets, until the houses gave way to open grass and bare trees. Willow skidded to a stop beneath a solitary horse chestnut, her breath coming out in thick white clouds.

'Home's the last place I need to be,' she said hoarsely. 'I need Solstice.'

She pressed her palm to the bark.

The tree split open like a seam, golden light spilling out so bright it hurt to look at. Jacen swore softly and shielded his eyes as they stepped through.

Warmth. Grass beneath their feet. A garden blooming impossibly out of season.

Willow swayed.

'I feel so cold, Jacen,' she murmured — and collapsed.

He caught her just in time, her weight sagging heavily against him. Snow drifted lazily around them as he looked up, heart hammering, and saw Taranis striding across the lawn, violet-blue eyes narrowing in concern.

He took Willow from Jacen without hesitation, frowning as icy power curled around her like mist.

'So,' he said grimly, 'what have you two been up to that she's channelling my power?'

'We were at school,' Jacen said, breathless. 'She said her head hurt. Then it started snowing.'

Inside the castle, Taranis laid Willow on a bed and pressed his fingers to her brow. The snow stopped at once. Colour crept back into her face — and then snapped away.

The cold vanished so abruptly it made her shudder.

Heat flooded her instead, fierce and feverish. Her cheeks flushed red, her skin burning.

'Don't touch her,' Taranis snapped, jerking his hand back. 'I need to make some calls.'

He left without another word.

Jacen sat on the edge of the bed, hands clenched in his lap. The air around Willow shimmered with heat. Meltwater dripped steadily onto the floor.

'Sorry,' she whispered.

He stared at his hands, still tingling where her skin had

burned him, and forced a smile. 'Hey. School was boring anyway.'

'I have ruined your weekend,' Willow wriggled as she got comfortable, her cheeks still flushed with heat.

'Nah, I can hang out with the lads,' his smile had his dimples popping. He moved his hand. He hesitated, then placed it back in

his lap.

'Jane likes you,'

'Yeah, I know,'

'You do?'

'Yeah,'

'So why don't you ask her out?'

'Well, the thing is, there is this other girl I like.'

'Really?'

'Yeah, she's odd but in the nicest way, and she can do all this cool

stuff,'

'Oh, Heli. She likes you too.'

'Not Heli. You,'

'I knew that. I like you as well,' Willow shut her eyes again.

'You sleep and we can do something next week.'

'I would like that–love you,'

'Love you too, my freaky nature girl.'

Time stretched.

Jacen pulled his phone from his pocket and unlocked it. No signal. He swore under his breath and tried again anyway, thumb tapping too hard at the screen.

His mum would have heard by now. The school always rang. He pictured her face — that tight, worried look she got when something was wrong and she didn't have all the information.

He typed a message he couldn't send. *I'm fine. I'm with*

Willow. Don't panic. He deleted it, then typed it again, staring at the empty signal bars like they might change if he looked hard enough.

Willow's breathing was shallow but steady. He watched her chest rise and fall, phone clutched uselessly in his hand, the heat from her skin warping the air between them.

There was nothing he could do. That didn't stop him checking again.

When Lilly appeared in the doorway, relief hit him so hard his chest ached.

'The school rang,' she said softly. 'Your mum's frantic.' Her gaze moved to Willow. 'Why did she come here?'

'She said she needed Solstice. Couldn't stop the snow.'

Lilly's gaze flicked to the phone clenched in Jacen's hand.

'Your mum?' she asked gently.

He nodded. 'No signal.'

'I've already called her,' Lilly said without fuss. 'She knows you're safe. She knows you're with me.'

The tension drained out of him all at once, leaving him light-headed.

'She asked me to tell you to ring when you can,' Lilly added, smiling. 'And to stop worrying.'

Jacen huffed out a shaky breath. 'That sounds like her.'

Taranis returned, looking grim. 'We had winter first. Now she's in summer. Don't touch her.'

Lilly ignored him. She laid a hand on Willow's forehead — and swayed, eyes fluttering, snatching her hand back just in time.

'Autumn,' she murmured, stifling a yawn. 'Spring next. Then she should wake.'

'She's too young for this,' Taranis said.

'I know.' Lilly rubbed her temples. 'She's gaining her Elder Council powers far too fast. Last week she burnt David by accident. I'm trying to find out why, but between human-caused disasters and the Council...' She trailed off.

'I'll take Jacen home,' she said finally.

Outside, Jacen hesitated, looking back at the castle.

'She isn't my Willow anymore, is she?'

Lilly's arms went around him. 'Oh, sweetheart. She loves you. She'll always need you.'

But as the tree closed behind them, the unease didn't lift.

Chapter Four

Solstice and Lilly were sitting in the small sitting room just off the main hall. This was Solstice's favourite room as it was cosy and warm, with a large window that faced onto the rose garden, a fire in the grate keeping the Scottish cold out. They had opened a bottle of wine while waiting for dinner when Andarta, Queen of Autumn, walked in. Her dark emerald, green eyes that perfectly complimented her dark red hair surveyed the two women, who sat smiling at her.

'Annie, what are you doing here?' Solstice exclaimed, moving to get her a glass and pouring the wine.

'Laran is still asleep, and Gail is still in London, and I was bored. Oh, David texted me, said he had something interesting to show me,' she smiled as Solstice passed her a glass of wine.

'Oh yeah, some odd plant in one of his greenhouses. Willow said she heard it calling to her and had a moment. Shook David up. He won't admit it, but I think it frightened him a bit,' Lilly explained.

Taking a sip, Andarta's gaze fell on Lilly. 'So, why are you here?' her abrupt manner made Lilly smile. Andarta was her most aloof queen, and it hadn't been until last year that Lilly had any social interactions with the prickly redhead.

'Willow is gaining her Elder Council powers,' Solstice replied while sipping her wine.

'Oh, what happened?' Andarta got comfortable, enjoying being included. She absently wondered why she didn't do this more often.

'She made it snow at school. Luckily Jacen brought her here,'

'Jacen? The human boy?'

'Yes, how do you know him?'

'Oh, I don't. Gail mentioned him. Your children made quite the impression on him,'

'Good, I hope,' Lilly smiled.

'Yes, I think their friendship will be a positive in his life. He has been very isolated while away at school and university.'

'Don't you mean get him away from that Eric?' Solstice chuckled.

'So, Willow, what other powers has she gained?'

'Well, she can already talk to the animals and influence plants. That was where she was going when we had the castle incident. She needed some advice from Rose,'

'Incident, that is the polite way of putting that escapade,' Solstice chuckled.

'I don't understand why this is happening. She is sixteen. Her body isn't ready for these powers yet. I was much older, and I got them one at a time, not all at once. This is happening much too fast,' Lilly said, rubbing her temples, trying to make the tiredness go away.

'Well, it is half term, so I can help her. Taranis enjoys having them stay. He enjoys William's company enormously.' Solstice poured more wine.

'Yes, William enjoys learning about the estate. He was looking at courses he could do while at university.'

'Oh, when is he going?'

'Starts in the autumn. he got into Edinburgh, so that's handy,'

'Oh yes, Taranis wants him to stay here. I told him he wouldn't want to do that if he was going to get the full university experience,' Solstice explained.

'Well, that's very kind of you to offer,' Lilly answered, feeling awkward in the face of such generous kindness.

'I heard Gail got the full university experience,' Solstice raised a brow, wondering if Andarta would reveal the trouble the boys got into.

'You heard about the jet incident,' Andarta mumbled.

'Yes, Anna told me she found it hilarious.'

'Laran didn't. He stopped Gail's allowance for a month,'

'What did he do?' Lilly gazed at the two women.

'He took Laran's jet so Eric could have a party on it.'

'Gosh, and he seems so sensible,'

'Oh, he is normally, but put him with Eric and they get into all sorts of trouble. Took Ashes helicopter just so they could go to a party across state,' Solstice giggled. 'Laran should never have taught that boy to fly.' Solstice slurped her wine to stop the giggles.

'Well, he had to do something after the car fiasco,'

'Car? Gail can drive?'

'Oh yes, built a car he found rusting in one of Harries barns when he was fourteen. Him and Eric used to go everywhere in it. Would have got away with it if there hadn't been a kidnap attempt on Gail,'

'That's awful,' Lilly gasped.

'We have had a few over the years. Humans are bonkers, the

lot of them,' Andarta shrugged. 'Gail still has the car Ash gifted to him when he passed his helicopter licence,'

'He asked for Willow's phone number. Maybe I shouldn't encourage that.'

'Did he!? That should be interesting.' Solstice poured more wine so she could hide her concern.

'I am sure he will behave like the perfect gentleman, Lilly,'

'Oh, it's not him I am worried about,' Lilly chuckled.

Gail studied the computer screen as he typed the final lines of his report. A gentle knock at the door had him glancing up.

'Come in,' he called.

The door opened to reveal Dahlia Veles. She stepped inside, brown eyes cast slightly downwards. Gail smiled. He admired Dahlia — efficient, organised, and precise. She ran the Autumn office with admirable competence, always impeccably dressed.

She was, of course, very attractive, with dark, curly auburn hair tumbling down her back, kept from her face by an Alice band, wisps framing her burnished-gold skin. Her manner towards him was respectful, a little shy, and, if he was honest, slightly intimidating.

'Your Highness,' she stuttered.

'Oh no, please — call me Gail.' Pushing to his feet, he walked around the desk and pulled out a chair for her. The blush that coloured her cheeks didn't escape his notice. 'How can I help?'

He sat back behind his desk, watching her. She was a little older than him, and if his upbringing had been more conventional, he suspected they might have been friends. As it was, all their interactions had always been professional.

'Um, well... as it's your last day, some of us wondered if you'd... well... like to come for a drink,' she blurted.

'Oh — sure, that would be lovely.' Gail smiled, noticing her blush deepen. His phone rang, rescuing him from the sudden awkwardness. 'Excuse me a moment.'

'Hello, Solstice — err, yes... now? Yes, of course.'

Putting the phone away, he glanced at Dahlia with regret. 'I'm sorry, I have to get to Scotland straight away. Family emergency. We'll have to rain-check tonight.'

'Right. That's okay. Maybe another time.'

He held the door for her. 'It's been a pleasure working with you.'

'And you,' she replied, offering her hand.

Once outside, Dahlia leaned against the wall to collect herself before slipping into her office, where she could watch him leave without him seeing her at all   and it wasn't just her physical presence he didn't seem to notice.

'Dahlia, what are you doing?' Althea's voice startled her.

'Oh — I didn't see you there,' Dahlia muttered, blushing as her eyes flicked to the opposite door.

Althea sidled up in time to see Gail walking away. 'Oh, I see.'

'He doesn't even know I exist,' Dahlia sighed, slumping into a vacant chair. 'Today was his last day.'

'So, ask him out for a drink.'

'I did. But he's got a family emergency and has gone to Scotland.'

'Oh,' was all Althea said.

Willow had been asleep but awoke feeling better—and hungry. After getting out of bed, she wrapped her gown around herself and headed to the kitchen. She picked up the kettle, took it to the sink, filled it with water, and set it back on its stand to boil. Willow decided she must be in Winter again; she was freezing.

Solstice had been helping her control these new powers, but Willow was finding it difficult and exhausting. They seemed to drain her. Making her tea, she hoped it would warm her up, as she was now absolutely icy. She tried not to shiver, but she could feel her body temperature dropping.

She cupped her cold hands around the mug, enjoying the warmth—until her hands became so cold that the tea froze in the cup, cracking it in half. Willow sighed, put the cup in the sink to thaw, and turned on the kettle to make another.

Taranis walked along the corridor, having finished the estate paperwork. He had decided he needed a coffee before tackling his duties as King of Winter. As he neared the kitchen, he immediately felt the temperature drop. He was alarmed to find a shivering Willow inside and the kitchen staff gathered in the hall.

'Sir, the Child of Nature needs your assistance,' his head chef said, stepping forward with a worried frown.

'Indeed. Um—why don't you all take the rest of the day off while I sort this?'

'Yes, sir, of course.' The head chef ushered his staff away.

'Willow, are you okay?' Taranis called.

'No. Not really,' came her shaky reply. He could hear the panic in her voice.

Taranis pushed the door open and stepped into what looked like a small snowstorm.

'Taranis, I can't stop the snow and I'm so cold and tired. I'm trying to make it warm, but I can't,' Willow said, trying not to panic.

'It's okay, Willow. Just concentrate—you can do this, sweetheart,' he soothed. The temperature continued to fall, a light frost spreading across the units and floor. It was snowing hard now, and the air had dropped well below zero. Willow sat on the floor shivering, looking utterly frozen and exhausted. Taranis knew this was bad—she could potentially freeze the entire castle and everyone in it.

He sat beside her, putting his arms around her and trying to absorb some of the power, but it wasn't enough. Taking out his phone, he dialled Solstice.

'Hi, honey. I, um—I have a situation with Willow. Could you come to the kitchen and bring William and David with you?' He hung up and turned back to Willow.

'Willow, honey, Solstice will be here soon. She's bringing William and your dad, okay? You need to try to warm up for them.'

'I'll try,' Willow whispered, her smile wobbling.

Solstice stepped out into the corridor, closing the kitchen door behind her before more heat escaped. The cold radiating from Willow was already seeping through to the hallway. Frost feathered up the walls, and the air tasted sharp, metallic.

Taranis is right. This could get dangerous very quickly. She pulled out her phone, her hands steady despite the rising urgency. Willow's shivering breaths still echoed in her mind.

Solstice exhaled once, then pressed Gail's number. He answered on the second ring.

'Hello, Solstice—'

'Gail, sweetheart, I'm sorry to trouble you,' she said, keeping her voice calm though a crack of ice sounded behind her. 'We've got a situation with Willow at the castle. Her Winter powers are flaring badly, and she's exhausted.'

She took a few steps away from the door as another flurry of snow drifted into the corridor.

'Is she hurt?' he asked immediately, all lightness gone from his

'Not hurt,' Solstice assured him, 'but she's very cold and losing control. She responds well to you, and having you here might help stabilise her. Could you come as soon as possible?' There was no hesitation.

'On my way.'

She closed her eyes in brief gratitude as the call ended. Then she slipped her phone into her pocket, squared her shoulders, and returned to the snow-filled kitchen.

'Willow, sweetheart—Solstice is here.' Relief was unmistakable in Taranis's voice.

'Hi, Solstice,' Willow shivered.

'Okay, honey, you need to concentrate. Close your eyes and think of a warm place.' Willow nodded.

'Good girl. Now imagine heat radiating outward,' Solstice suggested.

'I'm trying, Solstice, but I'm so tired.'

'I know, sweetheart,' Solstice murmured, kneeling on the ice- covered floor. Glancing up, her eyes met Taranis's. Evacuate the castle, she sent telepathically.

Taranis nodded, carefully getting to his feet and pulling out his phone to send the evacuation code.

Just then, perhaps the most beautiful boy Willow had ever seen walked in. Dressed in a dark grey suit that hugged his body, emphasising his broad shoulders and long, toned legs, his dark auburn hair was ruffled as if he had run his fingers through it. Dark, almost black eyes shone with humour and intelligence, set in a face that could easily grace a magazine cover—indeed, often did. His honey-toned skin gave him an exotic look. Willow knew exactly who he was; she had met him when she'd been held in this very castle by the Summer King. Her heart gave a small stumble. Gaillardia Aristata Autumn—Gail—heir to Autumn Enterprises and the Autumn King and Queen's son.

'Wow, guys, when did you put the ice rink in?' Gail joked as he stepped into the winter grotto of a kitchen. His eyes flicked to the fragile-looking girl on the floor, her mahogany hair shrouding her delicate shoulders as storm-cloud grey eyes met his. Willow Millbank, Child of Nature. Despite her frail appearance, he knew she was possibly the second most powerful person on the planet. Right now, she could kill every living thing in the castle. And you asked her out on a date—seriously, Autumn? the voice in his head mocked him.

'Well, you know me—always trying to improve the place,' Taranis laughed, pulling Gail into a hug, fully aware of what he was doing. 'Good to see you, Gail.'

'Hi, Solstice. How's it going?' Gail asked cheerfully, trying to hide how unnerved he was by Taranis's display of affection. He turned to the Queen of Winter, marvelling at her beauty as her glacial blue eyes smiled up at him from the floor beside Willow. She brushed her white hair back and hugged the girl.

'Not so good, is it, Willow?' Willow didn't answer, gripping Solstice's hand as she tried to stop the snow. Gail gave Willow a dazzling smile, noticing how pale, drawn, and exhausted she looked.

'Cup of tea, anyone?' he asked lightly, walking toward the kettle and taking care not to touch Willow—one accidental touch could freeze his blood and stop his heart. He had seen Solstice do it in battle; he knew how dangerous Willow's current state was.

'You hadn't forgotten I was staying this weekend, had you?'

Gail asked Taranis.

'No, of course not,' Solstice replied, smiling. 'Your usual room is ready.'

'Thanks. I was worried it might be the dungeon again,' Gail joked as Taranis blushed.

Willow watched him tease Taranis. He looked every inch the professional—and really hot, Willow thought, distracted. Her body temperature rose slightly without her noticing. Gail loosened his tie and unfastened the top button of his shirt.

Still shivering, Willow watched him check the kettle. She smiled at him—and the snow stopped.

'Good grief, it's cold in here. Oh good, you're putting the kettle on, Gail,' David remarked as he wandered in. He was dressed in his gardening clothes, which made Willow smile. Seeing her brother dressed the same only brightened her expression.

'Ah, this may take a while. Willow's been making iced tea again,' Gail said with a smirk. Willow chuckled, and the whole room brightened like a thousand sunbeams—instantly warmer.

'Could be worse. She could have been cooking. Now that would've been a disaster,' William quipped.

'Oh, you might have mentioned that before I started dating her,' Gail sighed dramatically, signing as he spoke so William could see.

'Hey! There is nothing wrong with my cooking!' Willow objected, automatically signing as well now that William was in the room—still impressed that Gail had bothered to learn it.

'Dating? I don't remember that being run past me,' David said sharply, glaring at Gail, who swallowed hard and went pale.

'I—yes, sir—I, um—' Gail stuttered as William burst out laughing.

'Dad, leave him alone,' Willow moaned.

'I'll fetch a bucket and mop, then,' Taranis said in relief as the ice began to melt. Solstice stood and smiled at everyone.

'Yeah, like you have any idea where the cleaning equipment is. Go find Trudy and her team—they're in the east wing,' Solstice said, turning to David and William.

'I sent the code,' Taranis admitted, looking sheepish as he realised he might have to do it himself.

'Well, you know Trudy—she never does what you ask. I think you'll find she's still in the east wing.' Solstice shooed him out as she followed David.

'David, are you staying for dinner?' she asked.

'Yeah, sure.'

'Can I touch you now?' Gail asked Willow hesitantly as he set the kettle back on its stand. He knew she could still hurt him. Willow nodded. He walked over to her and helped her up, wrapping his arms around her. He could feel how thin and cold she was through her wet pyjamas.

'Better?' he asked.

'Yes. Thank you,' Willow murmured, burying her head in his chest. The steady beat of his heart soothed her as she inhaled his familiar scent.

'You look really hot in that suit,' she muttered.

'Don't let your dad hear you say that,' Gail chuckled.

'Come on, let's get you into dry clothes and back to bed,' David said gently as he led them to Willow's room. Gail carried her easily.

'I love you, Dad,' she whispered.

'I love you too, sweetheart,' he chuckled. 'A hot bath and bed — that's what you need.' Gail set her down on her bed.

'I, um—I'll help William,' Gail said quickly, backing out, still uncomfortable around David.

Later, Gail found William in one of the smaller sitting rooms. 'You staying?' William asked.

'Yeah. I'm done with FERA and head back to Canada Monday. Thought I'd spend the weekend here.'

'I guess your date with Willow's off.'

'Yeah. I'd suggested the pub — something low-key. Get tomknow each other better. Not exactly an option now.'

'Come out with me tomorrow morning instead. Help the Rangers. Can you ride?'

'Yes. Rogers taught me as a kid,' Gail said, smiling faintly at the reminder of their shared world. 'So... date with Suzy. How did that go?'

William rolled his eyes, and the two of them settled in to gossip and catch up.

Chapter Five

Willow had woken early. She really hated sleeping alone. Climbing out of bed, she noticed sunshine glinting through the gap in the curtain. With a sigh, she slipped on her dressing gown and padded to the kitchen for a cup of tea, then wandered out to the terrace by the rose garden.

She sat with her mug, reflecting on yesterday. Her chances of going on a date with Gail were now smashed to pieces—so when he came strolling across the lawn, she nearly choked on her tea. Damn, he looked good in riding clothes.

'Bit early, isn't it, Willow?' he teased, flashing a devastating smile.

'I could say the same.'

'Oh yeah, I'm helping the rangers this morning. Meeting William—he asked me to join them last night,' Gail explained.

'How long are you staying here?' Willow asked, trying not to sound like she was prying.

'Just until I fly back to Canada on Monday. Thought I'd make myself useful,' he smiled again, sending butterflies through her stomach and a flicker of jealousy at her brother's easy friendship with him.

'Well, better go. Don't want to be late.'

'Gail... we are still friends, aren't we?' She fought to keep her voice steady, not needy.

'Yes... yes, of course. We can reschedule our date.'

'You still want to go out with me, then?' She glanced down at her feet.

'Yes—if you still want to. If you haven't changed your mind.'

'I'm going home later. Heli's back now... goodbye in advance in case I've already left when you get back,' she blurted, cheeks flushing.

'Oh, right. Well, I'd better go.' He bent and kissed her cheek.

'Gail—text me!'

'Sure. Stay safe.' He straightened and strode towards the stables.

Taranis' estate manager, Rogers, was a stout man with a ruddy complexion that spoke of a life outdoors. After being made redundant from a factory job, he'd changed careers and never looked back. He smiled as the two young men walked into the Gillies' office.

'Welcome, boys.' He quickly explained the day's jobs, speaking aloud while signing for William's benefit.

'Some villagers have reported poachers in the area. We'll form groups to check the stag and hind herds. Also...' He shuffled papers. 'We've had reports of mutilated carcasses. Rumours suggest a big cat. No collections have reported escapees, so we investigate with caution.'

'Are we taking the horses?'

'Yes. Some of the hinds are inaccessible by vehicle. Thomas, you and Clyde take the Land Rover. Everyone else—back here at 12.30 for lunch. Storm's forecast later.'

Rogers dismissed the rangers, then turned to William and Gail.

'Pleasure to see you again,' he said, shaking Gail's hand.

'Been a while,' Gail replied.

'Used to follow me round with more questions than I could answer—so I stuck him on a pony.'

'Loved every minute,' Gail chuckled.

'Right. Ride with Master William.'

They left the yard together, William grinning. He loved these early morning rides. With Gail opening their telepathic link, he could hear everything for once. It didn't take long to find the herd. They split up to check numbers.

'Right, William—you go right, I'll go left. Meet over the hill,' Gail called.

Gail breathed in the fresh, clean air and admired the sweep of the moor under the morning sun. In the distance, a second group of hinds caught his eye. He urged his horse into a canter, radioing Rogers with his position as he went. The heather brushed against his boots, the scent of it sharp in the warm air. For a moment, it was peaceful. Then his horse shied violently.

A ripple moved through the heather ahead — not the wind, but something deliberate. Gail leaned forward, murmuring reassurance to the animal, his gaze scanning for what had spooked it.

The 'tussocks' ahead shifted again, rising slowly until the truth of them emerged: figures, cloaked in camouflage that melted back into green and gold as they stepped clear.

Summer elves.

They came from all directions, boots whispering against the grass, until Gail realised they'd boxed him in. His horse tossed its head, ears flat, and Gail kept his voice low and calm, all the while counting them and noting the curve of their weapons. This wasn't a hunting party.

'Prince Autumn,' the lead elf said with a sneer. 'Always in the wrong place at the wrong time.'

Gail adjusted his grip on the reins, keeping his expression mild. 'So it would seem. What do you want?'

'You.'

His brow creased. 'Why?'

'I believe you're Prince Autumn. Or shall I call you Lord Aristata?' Gail gave a wry smile. 'I think you've confused me with someone else.'

The elf arched an eyebrow. 'Come, come. Even if you weren't who I think you are, we can't have you telling anyone we're here, now can we?'

That didn't ring true. Gail's mind ticked over fast. Why would a fully armed platoon of summer elves be out here in Winter territory? His disappearance would trigger a full-scale alert — surely they knew that. He let his eyes roam over their crossbows and rifles. Overkill, unless they were after something — or someone — else.

'What are you really doing up here?' he asked. 'Me being here was chance.'

'It wasn't you we wanted,' another elf said flatly. William. They were after William. But why?

'But you'll do,' the leader added with a smirk.

'Look, isn't this a bit extreme?' Gail kept his tone light, though his heart had kicked up a notch. 'You could have just knocked on the castle door and asked to talk to me.'

'Yes, because your father and uncle would have been so welcoming,' one of the others said with open sarcasm. The leader gave a sharp nod. A younger elf moved forward, reaching for Gail's leg to haul him down. Gail reacted on instinct — heels to the horse's sides, sending it surging forward in a burst of speed across the heather. Shouts and the crack of gunfire erupted behind him.

The horse leapt a ditch, and Gail felt the punch and burn of a bullet tearing past, one finding its mark. He gritted his teeth against the pain in his arm, clinging desperately to the reins. Another jump — and this time he lost his seat.

The world tilted. He hit the ground hard, pain exploding in his wrist, followed by the dull, muffled thump of his head striking one of the few rocks scattered across the moor. His helmet saved him from worse, but his vision blurred, black spots crowding in. He heard the pounding of retreating hoofbeats and the fading shouts of the elves — then nothing as he surrendered to the dark.

Turning his face up to the late afternoon sun, Rogers basked in the
tranquillity. They had been out here all day, and he had relished every second. This, he decided, was why he did this job. Urging his horse on, it was time to meet up with the two boys and start the long, leisurely trek back.

He pondered what was for dinner; moving here from Aberdeen had been the best decision he had ever made. Ambling along, caught up in various daydreams, it confused him to hear voices drifting across the moorland.

Rogers pulled his horse to a stop as he heard Gail's voice, his accent distinct. It had surprised Rogers that he enjoyed the boy's company as much as he did. The boys were intelligent and well- informed, understanding the difficulties in running the estate in the current climate. Looking up, he noticed clouds gathering on the tallest peak. Giving a sniff, he could feel the change in the weather.

Turning as William trotted up on his horse, a look of concern on his face, Rogers quickly signed that Gail was in some sort of trouble.

Slipping down off their horses, they crept forward on their bellies, letting the gorse and heather conceal their approach. He watched as men surrounded the young prince. William lay beside him, watching, before tapping him on the shoulder.

'What the hell are they doing on the estate?' William signed.

'No idea,' Rogers signed back. They watched as a brief exchange took place before Gail suddenly kicked his horse into a gallop.

Rogers and William scrambled back to their horses as the sound of gunfire rang across the valley. The elves giving chase while firing wildly.

Pulling his walkie-talkie out of his pocket, he radioed in their position and what he had found. Turning his horse, he headed after Gail. He notice the elves fall back. Concentrating on finding Gail he let the niggling worry about the elves and their motives slip to the back of his mind.

Jumping down even before his horse had stopped, Rogers ran to where Gail lay in the ditch. Kneeling, he felt for a pulse, relieved when he heard Gail groan.

'Laddie, we can't stay here. Can you ride?' Gail sat up slowly, wiping the blood from his eyes. Holding his hand up, he looked at the blood on his coat, confused.

'Laddie, we have to go,'

'I, yes, need to move... elves... lost my horse... my arm, they shot me,' his voice betraying his indignation. Gail opened his coat to inspect the wound.

'Let me see,' Rogers pulled away Gail's shirt to have a better look.

'Lucky it is just a graze. Your clothing and distance saved you. You are losing quite a lot of blood, and we need to get you somewhere so I can patch it up.'

'Yeah, lucky. Don't think I can ride,' Gail mumbled before passing out again.

'Okay... right... that would be a no then,' Rogers walked over to Gail's horse looping the reins back he walked it to where William was waiting patiently.

'There is a shepherd's hut across the moor. Do you know it, laddie?' He signed to William.

'Yes, I know the one,'

'I will bring Gail if you take his horse. I will meet you there. It is too late to get back now, okay?'

'Okay, meet you there,' William signed back, turning the horses he rode away.

'Taranis,' Solstice pushed open the door. 'Where are the boys?'

Taranis turned his gaze away from the computer screen and the estate accounts to glance at Solstice.

'Um, up on the moor with the rangers. You know how William enjoys helping.'

'Did Gail go with them?'

'Yeah, I think so. He enjoys Rogers' company and Williams. Why?' He watched as Solstice slumped into a chair.

'He likes her.' Solstice turned her gaze to the garden outside.

'Who?' Taranis asked confused at the change.

'Willow, he likes her,'

'Of course he does, she is a lovely girl,'

'I promised Jasmine that he wouldn't meet her, and now he has and to be honest, that is partly your fault,'

'Solstice, honey,' Taranis moved from his chair and knelt before his wife, taking her hands in his.

'You haven't let her down. He is happy and healthy and young. Of course, he likes her. He is a boy, and she is a pretty girl, the sister of

his friend,' Taranis reasoned.

'But the prophecy, what he could become ... and her powers are so out of control,' Taranis sat back in his chair.

'That book Jasmine found is superstitious nonsense. Written in the dark ages for goodness sake. I seem to recall I saved you twice from being burned as a witch, back when that book was written,' Taranis answered patiently trying to inject some humour.

'I know but I still worry. What if it isn't?'

'This is the modern world. He is fine, perfectly normal. Andarta has done an excellent job of bringing him up. As for Willow, she is

Child of Nature. I have talked to Lilly. She thinks this is down to global warming. Willow is reflecting that. She will need to be a different Mother Nature to combat the mess the Humans are making.

We talked about this,'

'I know, it's just I worry about him. Jasmine was my best friend, and I lost her and then Gail to Annie. I know it was for the best, but...'

'Sweetheart, you were a fantastic friend, and you didn't lose him.

He is an autumn elf. He had to go to Annie to keep him

safe,' Taranis sighed. They had had these conversations in different forms many times over the years.

'What if Laran finds out?'

'He won't,'

'How can you be sure?'

'Annie is very thorough she knows what he is and what he could be. She will always protect Gail from Laran. Laran loves the boy. He would never hurt him. Apart from us and Annie, no one else knows, okay? He is safe. Besides, if Gail dates Willow, that will be the last thing that could hurt him,' Taranis gave a chuckle to ease the tension.

'Yes, you are right. They are young, and Annie would never allow harm to come to him. Sorry, I worry too much,'

'No, you don't. You loved his mother, I get that. It is good to look out for him. Hyperion should not have involved him, but you know how he likes to annoy Laran.' Taranis turned to the door as a soft knock interrupted them.

'Come in,' he called for a winter elf to push open the door.

'Sir, there has been an incident up on the moor. You are needed urgently.'

'Thank you. I will be there shortly,' Taranis turned back to Solstice.

'Right, shall we see what trouble those children have got into this time?' A smile pulled at his lips despite the levity of the situation. He held out his hand to Solstice as she climbed to her feet.

'It would seem I misdirected my concerns,'

'So it would seem,' Taranis remarked as they left the office and headed to the rangers' station.

Rogers lifted Gail and settled him across his own mount, holding him steady.

The rain had started by the time they reached the long, turf-roofed hut. Inside, Rogers laid Gail on the sofa, got the fire going, and began tending the wounds. By the time William came in, bolting the door, the storm was a steady roar outside.

'Sorry,' Gail murmured.

'It's alright. I've radioed in — they know where we are.' Rogers handed him water and painkillers, watching as he drifted in and out.

William crouched beside him, signing, How are you?

'Been better,' Gail said faintly, the link between them letting William hear his voice.

'So, you like the wee lassie.'

'How do you know that?' Gail answered, his speech slow.

'I am old, not blind.'

'Yeah, I like her, not sure how much she likes me though.' Gail closed his eyes.

'Stay awake.'

'Trying... to.'

'She likes you a lot,' William chuckled .

'Here,' Rogers pulled a whiskey bottle from a cupboard and poured a small amount into a cup, which he knocked back before pouring some more and putting it to Gail's lips. 'Drink,' he instructed. Gail swallowed and then coughed.

'Does everyone have Taranis' whiskey?' William asked.

'Probably. He doesn't sell it, just gives it away, the daft man,' Rogers laughed.

'Taranis, he got me very drunk once...'

'Did he now?' said Rogers, giving Gail another slug of whiskey.

'Yeah, mum was very cross with him.' Gail's voice faded as his eyes

drifted shut.

'Stay awake, laddie.'

'Yeah... cold though, and tired.'

'I know, but we have to stay here overnight. Now, tell me why you don't think the lassie likes you, hmm.'

'She didn't seem upset our date got cancelled. I am not very good with girls,'

'When did you talk to her?' William asked.

'Oh, I went and said goodnight last night it was still snowing in her room your mum was there.'

'Trust me she likes you a lot. Besides it isn't as if she cancelled it. It was more the circumstances of her current situation,' William answered from where he was curled in a large armchair drinking his soup.

'Stay awake,' Rogers put more logs on the fire and found another blanket, checking the bullet wound and taking Gail's pulse.

'That makes two of us I am not very good with girls either,' William said.

'Is it bad?' William bit his lip while looking at Gail's pale sweaty face.

'He will be fine once we get him to a doctor,' Rogers reassured William. They didn't have long to talk before the first knock came —hard, sharp, and wrong. Rogers' hand went to the gun at his side.

The knock came again — not a polite rap, but the solid thump of someone who already thought they had the right to be inside.

'Open up,' a voice called. It wasn't one Rogers recognised. He slipped the radio from his pocket, thumbing it to life.

'Castle One, copy.' His voice was low, calm. At the same time, he signed to William: Get to Gail's side.

'Open the door now or we'll use force,' the voice outside threatened.

The radio crackled. 'Castle One to Ranger One, report your position and situation,' Taranis's voice came through, distorted by the static.

'Castle One, we're in the barn,' Rogers replied evenly, his tone carrying the code phrase. 'One sheep hurt. Wolves at the door. Require assistance.'

William's eyes widened at the phrasing — wolves meant hostile elves. You open it, then move back, Rogers signed. William gave a sharp nod, undoing the bolt and pulling the door open before stepping quickly in front of Gail.

Four summer elves shouldered their way inside, dripping rainwater onto the wooden floor. Their weapons stayed in their hands, muzzles angled low but ready. They scanned the room in quick, practiced sweeps before their eyes fixed on the sofa.

'I knew I hit him,' one muttered with grim satisfaction. The leader, taller than the rest and with his gold hair tied back in a warrior's braid, nodded towards the sofa. 'Prince Autumn. How badly is he hurt?' he asked William.

'Broken wrist, head knock, bullet graze,' Rogers answered for him, his voice flat.

'So he's not going to cause trouble?'

'Unlikely.'

The leader's gaze flicked to William. 'And you, boy? Going to give us any problems?' William stared at him blankly, as if the words had no meaning.

'He's deaf,' Rogers said, adding the signs so William could

follow the exchange. The elf's lip curled. 'No wonder the Autumn King hid the
   child.'

Gail stirred, pushing himself up on the sofa with a grunt of pain. His eyes were fever-bright, his good hand cradling his injured wrist. 'You seem well informed about my family.'

The leader didn't deny it. 'I know your kind don't like imperfection. Better to parade a war orphan as heir than acknowledge your own blood.'

'You seem very sure of yourself,' Gail said quietly. 'And you seem to know my name. But if you know me that well, you'll know I'm in no position to threaten you.'

'Indeed. Your father's in hibernation, but nice try.'

'Maybe so,' Gail allowed, 'but my uncle isn't — and when he learns there are armed summer elves in his territory, he won't be happy.'

The elf gave a faint smile. 'We'll be gone before he gets here. We want you and the deaf boy.'

'Why? Who sent you?'

'You'll find out soon enough.'

Rogers stepped slightly in front of the boys, forcing the leader to shift his gaze. 'He needs a healer. That bullet wound's deeper than it looks.'

'He'll get the best care once the storm passes,' the elf said, tone making it clear "care" meant whatever suited them.

Outside, the rain hammered on the turf roof, wind rattling the shutters. Inside, the room had shifted — the summer elves positioning themselves by doors and windows, two with rifles trained on the sofa. William sank into a chair next to Gail, careful to keep his hands low.

They already hurt you, he signed, the movements hidden from view.

'They won't... kill us,' Gail whispered back, but the doubt in his voice betrayed him. Rogers met William's eye. The look said everything: Trust Taranis. Hold on.

Gail's breathing steadied, though his eyes were half-lidded with exhaustion. William tucked himself deeper into his seat, the crackle of the fire and the hiss of rain outside wrapping the little hut in a tense, waiting silence.

Chapter Six

Taranis's study smelled faintly of wood polish and coffee, the air warm from the low hum of a space heater tucked under the big bay window. One wall was lined with shelves of leather-bound volumes, relics from centuries past; the opposite wall was dominated by twin widescreen montors glowing with real-time maps of the moor. The old and new sat side by side — a battered oak table strewn with handwritten notes, a drone controller resting beside a brass compass, a steaming mug perched precariously atop an ancient atlas.

Outside, rain slicked the mullioned glass, the occasional gust rattling the frames. Taranis stood over the map spread across the desk, fingertips braced on either side. His eyes traced the contour lines as if he could see through them to the boys' exact location.

'What do they want?' His voice was quiet but carried across the room to Lord Aquillo, who leaned against the corner of the desk with a tablet in hand, scrolling through satellite images.

He looked up at Lord Aquillo, the youngest of the Winter

lords. Orphaned at a young age, Taranis had practically raised him. Now Aquillo acted as Taranis's right hand.

'Best guess is the young Autumn Prince,'

'Gail, hmm. Queen Autumn must be mad as hell with all the attention Gail is getting,'

'Indeed,' Taranis responded pensively. Why was Gail hidden away? What was she hiding? Why did King Summer really take the boy?

Taranis didn't for one minute believe it was just to annoy Laran. What-ever Hyperion's motives, it seemed his grand scheme was beginning to unravel. And Gail seemed to be at the centre of everything. 'Do you believe in coincidences?' Taranis turned his attention on young Aquillo.

'No, my King, I do not.'

'Ever noticed anything different with Gail?'

Aquillo laughed. 'What, apart from the genius level intelligence, or that he can fly and fix any machine. Or that even though his surrogate father is King Autumn, renowned butcher, Gail has managed to come out relatively well adjusted.' Aquillo shrugged. Taranis chuckled under his breath.

The door burst open.

'The boys — they're in trouble!' Willow stood there, hair wild from her rush, cheeks flushed.

'I know, sweetheart,' Taranis said, coming around the desk.

'I'm doing everything I can to get them back.'

'Willow, why are you out of bed?' Lilly's voice followed her in. She held her phone like a compass, a tracking app glowing on the screen.

'Mum, I can feel it. Something's wrong.'

'I know.' Lilly slipped an arm around her daughter's shoulders. 'Now you've got the power of the seasons, Autumn's pull is stronger. You feel William — and through him, Gail. Like a thread tugging at you.'

She moved to the desk, eyes on the map. 'That's rough country for moving troops.'

'Not if you drop a storm right over them,' Taranis said. 'My rangers can ride in under the weather cover. Once they're close, you bring enough thunder to hide the helicopter.'

Lilly considered. 'That could work. Send me your GPS pings.'

'Already on your phone.'

Willow stepped forward. 'What about me? And don't say "wait here".'

'Can you ride?'

'Yes.'

'Then you go with the rangers. No room in the chopper.' Aquillo inclined his head, stepping forward. 'Child of Nature, it would be my honour if you rode with me.'

Willow nearly smiled. He looked like he belonged in a painting — silver-white hair, ice-blue eyes — but the radio clipped to his jacket and tactical gloves hanging from his belt brought the present day sharply back.

'It's a pleasure,' she said. 'I'll change and meet you at the stables.'

The ride over the moor was a battle against the elements. Rain sheeted sideways, stinging any exposed skin, and the ground was a patchwork of sodden heather and hidden hollows.

The rangers' helmet lamps cut narrow paths through the storm, their horses' breath steaming in the cold.

Willow leaned low over her mare's neck, her coat pulled tight, hair plastered damp to her face. Beside her, Aquillo rode with calm assurance, the grey under him picking its way over the uneven ground. Overhead, Lilly's storm swirled — black clouds roiling like an ocean in the sky, occasional forks of lightning splitting the darkness.

'There!' The lead ranger's voice crackled in her earpiece.

Through the rain, she made out the long, low turf-roofed hut crouched against the wind, its windows yellow with lamplight.

'Soldiers go in first,' Aquillo said, reining closer so she could hear. 'We hold the perimeter. Catch anyone trying to run.' His hand rested on the stock of the shotgun across his back. Thunder rolled so close it rattled in her chest.

Inside the hut, the air was thick with woodsmoke and the sharp tang of antiseptic. The log burner's heat didn't quite chase away the damp that clung to every surface. Gail lay swaddled in a fleece blanket on the sagging leather sofa, skin pale, hair damp with sweat. Rogers knelt beside him, dabbing his forehead with a cloth from the open first-aid kit on the coffee table.

'He's worse, isn't he?' William asked quietly.

'Aye. He needs a hospital.' The lead summer elf stepped forward, rifle angled casually at the floor but eyes sharp. 'Time to move.' William blocked his path. 'He's too sick to—'

The shove sent him stumbling into the side table, the mug there clattering to the floor.

'It's alright, laddie,' Rogers murmured, lifting Gail into his arms. Cold air punched into the room as the door was opened.

'Rogers,' Gail whispered, voice barely audible, 'on my mark — drop me.' His good hand slid under the blanket, fingers closing on the grip of Rogers's pistol.

'Now.'

Rogers let go. Gail hit the floor firing — the muffled cracks almost lost in the thunder outside. 'Drop William!' he shouted, pivoting to fire again.

An elf slammed into him, wrenching his broken wrist until pain exploded white-hot.

'I knew you'd be trouble,' the elf growled, punching him in the shoulder wound.

Outside, the helicopter came in low, a black silhouette against the lightning. Rotor wash tore at the grass, rain whipping sideways, but the storm masked the noise. Soldiers in plate carriers and NVGs fast-roped down, boots splashing into mud.

The breaching ram smashed the door. A flashbang rolled inside — a blinding white flare and deafening crack. Gail dropped flat, Rogers hauling William down beside him.

The elves hesitated just long enough for the Benelli's bark to drop their leader; the staccato chatter of MP5s cut through the rest. Aquillo and the rangers came in behind the soldiers.

'The laddie's injured,' Rogers said, straightening.

'Get him to the helicopter,' Aquillo ordered.

'I can walk,' Gail muttered, leaning on Rogers all the same.

'Load them up,' Aquillo told the sergeant. 'Willow and I will ride back. Rangers handle clean-up.'

Willow stood in the churned mud, hair whipping across her face, watching as Gail, William, and Rogers were lifted aboard.

The ramp closed, the rotors thundered, and the helicopter rose into the storm.

Almost at once, the rain eased. The clouds began to fray at the edges, revealing the faintest line of orange where the sun would soon rise.

The helicopter's interior smelled of oil, metal, and damp wool. Gail sat slumped against Rogers, his eyes half-lidded, pale in the dim red cabin lights. William kept one hand on his friends knee, the other gripping the seat strap so tightly his knuckles were white.

Through the headset, the crew's clipped voices were barely audible over the rotors. Outside, the moor unrolled in dark, sodden patches until the first glint of the castle's floodlights broke through the mist.

'Five minutes,' the crew chief signalled with a raised hand. By the time they touched down in the courtyard, Taranis was already there, coat collar up against the wind, Solstice at his side.

The blades sent a wash of grit and rain swirling around them as the soldiers jumped down. Rogers came last, still half-carrying Gail.

'Inside, now,' Taranis ordered, his voice low but sharp. The castle swallowed them — warmth replacing the night's cold. Boots squeaked on the tiled floor. Staff stepped aside, eyes wide, murmuring as the group passed.

In the great hall, the fire roared, heat shimmering against the stone walls. Solstice was already moving, peeling Gail's wet coat away with practiced care, her fingers finding the edge of the bandage.

'Bullet graze, broken wrist, mild concussion,' Rogers reported.

'Mild?' Gail tried for a smirk, but it came out more as a grimace.

'You're lucky you didn't lose the arm,' Rogers replied dryly. Willow appeared at the edge of the crowd, cheeks flushed from the ride back. She hesitated for half a breath before crossing the hall, ignoring the way her legs still trembled from cold and adrenaline.

'You're alive,' she said softly, eyes fixed on Gail's face.

'Told you we'd reschedule,' he murmured, and the crooked half-smile almost undid her. William stepped in, looping an arm briefly around her shoulders before leaning in toward Gail. 'You look like crap.'

'Thanks, feel it,' Gail shot back. The tension in the room eased a fraction.

Solstice waved toward the corridor. 'Infirmary. Now.'

As the little group moved off, Taranis lingered by the fire, his gaze following them until they disappeared from sight. Beside him, Solstice exhaled slowly.

'That could have gone much worse,' she murmured.

'It still might,' Taranis replied quietly, eyes shifting toward the window where the storm had finally broken, leaving only streaks of pale gold in the dawn sky.

They had barely disappeared down the infirmary corridor

when Rogers returned from handing over his soaked coat to a passing maid. His boots left faint prints on the flagstones as he crossed to Taranis, who was still staring into the fire as though it held answers.

'You'll want to know,' Rogers began in a low voice, 'it wasn't just Gail they were after.'

Taranis's head turned sharply. 'William?'

Rogers nodded once. 'They asked for "the deaf boy" like they'd been told about him in detail. The way they said it… like he was a prize they'd been sent to collect.'

The Winter King's jaw tightened. 'And they were summer elves?'

'Armed. Organised. Not just a stray hunting party — they knew exactly where to find us.' Rogers glanced toward the shadowed corridor, where the echo of Solstice's voice still drifted faintly.

'They didn't care about being seen either. That's what bothers me.'

Taranis's gaze went to the rain-slick window, the last streaks of gold now fading to a pale, ordinary morning. 'It means they wanted to be noticed.'

'Or,' Rogers said, his voice quieter still, 'they wanted to send a message.'

The fire cracked loudly between them, throwing sparks into the air. Somewhere deeper in the castle, a door slammed against stone, and the sound carried in the silence that followed.

Taranis didn't look away from the flames. 'Find out where they came from, Rogers. And how close they got before we saw them.'

Rogers inclined his head. 'Aye, my King.'

Chapter Seven

The winter light through the high castle windows felt thin, the sky outside heavy with the last scraps of storm cloud. Gail sat on the edge of the infirmary bed, still pale but stubbornly upright, his wrist in a neat white cast. Taranis leaned against the stone wall opposite, arms folded, his expression unreadable.

'We were being watched,' Gail said, breaking the silence.

'Before the gunfire, before they even came out of the heather... they knew exactly where we'd be.'

Andarta, perched on the chair beside him, exchanged a glance with Taranis. 'Could they have followed you from the castle?'

'Not a chance,' Rogers said from the corner, where he was dismantling a rifle for cleaning. 'We'd have spotted a tail before we left the grounds. They were already out there.'

William signed quickly from his own seat, and Gail translated without hesitation. 'He says they called me "Prince Autumn" right away. Didn't even ask my name.' That made Taranis look up sharply. 'So they weren't guessing.'

'No,' Gail replied. 'And they knew about William too.

Called him "the deaf boy" like it was supposed to mean something.'

Willow frowned. 'Why would they want you two? Together?'

'That,' Taranis said, 'is the question. Summer elves don't make random grabs. If they've crossed into winter territory with guns, they've been sent.'

'By who?' Willow pressed.

'That's what I intend to find out,' Taranis replied. 'Until we do, neither of you goes anywhere without protection.'

'I'm not going to be babysat,' Gail muttered.

'It's not babysitting,' Taranis said evenly. 'It's making sure you're alive tomorrow.'

A long pause followed, broken only by the hiss of the radiator and the faint clang of a kitchen trolley down the corridor.

'The Dark Elves have been unusually quiet,' Andarta said at last. 'I don't like it.' She glanced at Taranis. 'You'll share what your scouts turn up?'

'You'll have it before you leave,' Taranis promised.

Gail gave her a sideways look. 'So... we are leaving?'

'Yes. I'm taking you home to Canada,' she said. 'Your father will want to hear about this in person, and you need more rest than you'll get here.'

Taranis straightened from the wall. 'Fair enough. Rogers will get you to the tree circle.'

They said their goodbyes in the west courtyard, boots crunching on gravel still wet from the morning's rain. Lilly was already there with Willow and William, ready to step through a second tree back to Dorset. She caught Andarta's eye.

'Safe journey,' Lilly said.

'And you,' Andarta replied.

The great oak trunks in the courtyard shimmered faintly, the bark rippling like disturbed water. Andarta took Gail's good arm, and together they stepped forward into the cool green glow.

Warm air and the scent of pine greeted them as they stepped out into the familiar woods behind their Canadian home. Snow lay in a soft crust across the garden, the cedar rooflines white against the deep blue of the sky.

By the time they had shed coats and boots, the kitchen smelled of fresh coffee.

Laran's mind stirred first, registering warmth, muted light, and the faint sound of voices somewhere down the hall. He forced his eyes open. He knew he was home, though he had no idea how long he had been in hibernation.

He lay still, listening to the quiet rhythm of the house. His heart, slow from long healing sleep, began to climb towards normal. As King of the Autumn Elves, hibernation was one of the gifts that had kept him alive for millennia, allowing his body to repair itself far more rapidly than any mortal's.

A nurse entered the room, checking the monitors and the drip in his arm.

'How do you feel, sir?' she asked politely.

'I feel fine. Sore.'

Once she had left, Laran gathered himself and pushed upright. A dizzy spell washed over him, but he waited until it passed before making his way into the bathroom. The shower's warmth eased the final fog from his senses. Dressed at last, he walked slowly down the hall towards the kitchen, drawn by the sound of Gail and Andarta talking.

He paused in the doorway, leaning on the frame. 'What did I miss?'

Andarta looked up from the island, where she and Gail were bent over a map spread across the marble.

'Quite a lot,' she said. 'And none of it good.'

Laran crossed the kitchen and eased himself onto the stool beside Gail. The younger elf hesitated, unsure where to begin.

'We were ambushed on the moor,' Gail said at last. 'They knew exactly who we were — called me "Prince Autumn" and William "the deaf boy". It wasn't random.'

Laran's gaze sharpened. 'Did they say what they wanted?'

'Not exactly,' Gail replied. 'But it was planned.'

Andarta gave a humourless laugh. 'Summer elves with guns, Laran. Crossing into winter territory. And it wasn't Hyperion this time.'

Laran exhaled sharply, then shifted the subject. 'What happened at the castle? Is everyone all right?'

'Where shall I start?'

'Oh — it went that well, then?'

'Yeah... well, sort of,' Gail admitted, already regretting mentioning it.

'Start with the siege,' Laran said, smiling at Gail's expression of regret.

'Well... everyone who matters is all right. Hyperion must have decided he really enjoyed stabbing people, because Taranis got it as well. Honestly, Hyperion should've stayed in exile. Going around stabbing people isn't exactly a great comeback plan,' Gail said, pulling a face.

Laran laughed — then immediately regretted it as pain tore across his healing side. 'Please don't make me laugh.'

'Oh — sorry,' Gail said quickly.

'Is Taranis all right now?' Laran asked.

'Yeah, he's fine. Actually, it kind of helped. Solstice spent a few weeks nursing him back to health, and now their marriage is stronger than ever.'

'Oh! Good. Maybe she's cheered up. She had a right go at me the other — well, month, I think,' Laran muttered, settling himself more comfortably.

'What happened to Hyperion? How did they stop him?' he asked.

'Alectrona showed up at the last second,' Gail said. 'Gave him a proper telling-off. He's at FERA now.'

Laran's eyes drifted to Gail's wrist. 'Your wrist — was that from the ambush?'

'Yeah. I fell off my horse when one of them shot me.'

Laran's frown was one of fear, not surprise. 'I'm sorry, Gail. I knew they'd come for you, but not that it was that close.'

'Yeah. I was out with William and the rangers. They were after me and William specifically.'

'Did they give any indication why?' Laran asked, voice tight.

'Not really. Dad — let me finish.'

'Sorry. Go on.'

'Lilly knows you know about my link to William. She was really understanding — told us to keep it quiet. William's nice. Put up a right fight at the end. They both did — him and Willow.' Gail opened the fridge and took out an onion, peeling it as he spoke.

'They were brilliant when we were locked in the castle. Willow's very pretty,' he added, chopping the onion. 'Brave, funny — she teases William constantly. And me. I was supposed to see her a couple of weekends ago, but she froze the castle, so I ended up riding with William instead. It was great... right until I got shot and fell off my horse. Broke my wrist. Cast comes off next week — they're putting a lighter one on.'

He tipped the chopped onion into a pan.

'These elves on the moor,' Laran said, brows drawn. 'They

knew far too much. About you. About William. About me. That wasn't chance.'

'Exactly. They even knew I was trained by Hàlfr.'

'Really? I'll speak to Hàlfr.'

'I've submitted a report,' Gail said. He stirred the onions and tipped in tomatoes. 'Taranis and Lilly came to the rescue. Frosty met Willow.'

'Frosty?'

'Xavier Aquillo.'

'How did that go?'

'He likes her. Obviously,' Gail muttered, as Laran smirked.

'Why was William at the castle?' Laran asked, storing the information away for a later conversation with Lilly.

'Oh... him and David were helping Solstice fix the rose garden and plan Chelsea. I was going on a date with Willow. Had to ask David's permission. It was so embarrassing.' Gail blushed.

'I love their English accents, though. When she froze the castle, the date was cancelled. She's got it under control now — according to William — though he's fed up with her freezing random things.'

Realising he'd said too much, Gail quickly asked, 'Do you want a drink? There's beer in the fridge, or wine.'

'Beer would be fine,' Laran said, amused by the blush. Gail dating Willow. This should be interesting.

'Dad,' Gail began cautiously as he handed over the beer. 'I noticed something at the castle. About my link to William.'

'Oh? And what was that?'

'Er... William looks just like you.'

'Does he? I hadn't noticed. How odd,' Laran replied far too casually.

'The elves who held us — they said things. About you and William.'

'They were trying to rile you up, Gail. You know the tactics.'

'So it's just a coincidence?' Gail asked, disbelief clear.

'Yeah, of course it is. What sort of question is that?' Laran snapped.

'Sorry. Stupid question. You just... look very similar. Anyway — forget I said anything.' Gail hesitated, then blurted, 'It's just... why am I linked to him?'

'Gail — drop it,' Laran murmured, a menacing edge to his voice making it perfectly clear the conversation was over. Gail's phone buzzed sharply against the marble. He picked it up, glanced at the screen, and went rigid. 'It's from Willow.

William can't breathe. House on fire.'

The words seemed to hit Gail like a physical blow. He sucked in a breath that didn't quite reach his lungs, a hand flying to his chest. 'I... can't...' The sentence broke apart as a violent cough tore through him. He slid off the stool, knees hitting the tiles, fighting for air.

'Gail!' Andarta dropped to the floor with him, one arm round his shoulders. 'Laran, the nurse — now.'

Laran was already moving. By the time he returned with the nurse and an oxygen cylinder, Gail's breaths were shallow and panicked, his face grey. They got the mask over his mouth and nose; the nurse checked his pulse, brisk and calm despite the urgency.

Gail's breathing had steadied, the oxygen mask still in place as Andarta sat beside him, holding his hand. His skin was clammy, his eyes half-lidded, but there was more colour in his cheeks than there had been minutes ago.

'It's easing,' he rasped, voice still rough.

'You're not going anywhere,' Andarta said firmly. 'Whatever's happening to William, you're too linked to risk moving until the nurse says so.'

From the doorway, Laran nodded in agreement. 'She's right.

Stay with him. If he takes another hit through the bond, you need to be here — not halfway across the world.'

Andarta narrowed her eyes. 'And you? Charging off still half-healed?'

'Someone has to get to Lilly. You've got your hands full.' He crossed to the bed, resting a hand lightly on Gail's uninjured shoulder. 'I'll send word when I know more. You focus on keeping him breathing.'

Gail tried to smirk but ended up coughing again. 'Don't... get stabbed this time.'

'No promises,' Laran replied, but there was a flicker of a smile before he turned, pulling on his coat. A moment later, the old spruce in the back garden flared with green-gold light — and he was gone.

Chapter Eight

W illow woke with a start. She rubbed her eyes and glanced around her bedroom in panic. The fire alarm was going off, and she could smell smoke.

'Heli, wake up, the house is on fire,' Willow said as she got out of bed. She wrapped a sheet round them both and opened the door to her bedroom. The hall leading to her parents' room was full of smoke and pitch black. Willow coughed and spluttered as she felt her way along, desperately hoping that her parents were okay.

David was already up and coughing. He pulled on his jeans and woke Lilly, who leapt out of bed like a scalded cat. Pulling the bedroom door open to see Willow and Heli groping along the hall towards him, both wearing an expression of terror.

'Willow, get out, use the landing window like we practised. Climb down by the front door and wait on the lawn. Lilly, go with her while I get William,' he shouted above the noise of the fire alarm.

Lilly had grabbed the sheet off the bed and wrapped it around herself as she ushered Willow toward the upstairs hall window. She could hear the crackle of flames coming from downstairs and could feel the heat of the fire as it licked its way up the walls and banister towards them. Lilly lifted her hands and blasted ice- cold air and rain, but it wasn't enough. She opened the window and let Willow and Heli climb down. She climbed down after them and, reaching the ground, dialled the emergency services on her mobile phone.

David ran across the landing to William's room. Since he was deaf, he wouldn't have heard the alarm. Althea was already on William's bed, and the smoke hung in the air, thick. William had black smears around his nose, evidence of where he had breathed the toxic smoke in. Althea was sitting on his chest, shaking him.

'I can't wake him,' she cried.

'Don't worry, Althea. Just get out. I'll bring him. The girls have already climbed out of the landing window. They will help you,' said David, picking the now unconscious William up and following Althea down the hall.

When they got to the window, the fire brigade was already there. Jacen had seen the smoke when he went to milk the cows and had phoned the fire service. Two firefighters helped David with William, and once they were safely on the lawn, they started giving William CPR. Lilly and Willow stood, clinging to each other as they watched, completely stunned. Eventually, William coughed and opened his eyes. Lilly ran over to him and hugged him, tears of relief streaming down her face.

The ambulance arrived, and they put William inside. He had to be taken to hospital to ensure that the smoke had done no lasting damage to his lungs. David went with them. Sarah, Jacen's mum, arrived to take Willow back to their house. Heli had gone with Willow and Althea said that she was going to inform Rose and Tammy of what had happened. Lilly stood alone on the lawn, shocked and traumatised, watching as the fire brigade swarmed around her once beautiful cottage.

Chapter Nine

'iss, are you okay?' The chief firefighter gazed at
the fragile woman in front of him.

'Yes, sorry, you were saying?' Lilly pulled
herself back to the conversation.

'We will return with the investigation team in a couple of
days once the heat has dissipated.'

'Oh, yes. Thank you.'

'Miss, is there someone I should call?'

'Oh, no, I will go to my grandmother's in a bit,' she said,
forcing a small smile. The firefighter's concern faded, but not
entirely.

'If you are sure.'

'Yes, please don't let me detain you any longer.'

She stood shivering in her pyjamas as the fire engine's lights
dwindled along the lane. Her phone felt heavy in her cold-
numbed hands. It was five o'clock in the morning, and she had
never felt so alone. Relief almost floored her when she saw a
figure striding up the garden path.

Laran's expression was all shock and concern as he took in

the ruin. The roof had caved in, dragging the chimneys down with it. Half the back wall was gone entirely. The air still smelt of wet ash. Lilly looked smaller than he remembered, streaked with soot, two clean lines of tears cutting through the grime.

He placed his hands on her shoulders, gently turning her away from the wreckage. 'Please, Lilly, you can't stay here. I'm taking you to Rose's.'

He kept his voice calm, though his ribs protested at the thought. She was deep in shock — he'd seen that look too often in soldiers — and there would be no coaxing her into movement.

With a quiet breath, he lifted her into his arms, gritting his teeth against the stab of pain in his side, and carried her towards the oak at the garden's edge.

The bark warmed under his palm. Light rippled up the trunk. Lilly rested her head against his shoulder and closed her eyes.

Finally, she felt safe.

Laran stepped into Rose's hallway and went straight upstairs, laying Lilly in the spare bed. She didn't stir. When he came back down, Rose was already in the kitchen. She slid a mug of coffee towards him without a word.

'Good to see you too, Rose,' he said, sitting opposite her.

'When did you wake up?' she asked, scanning his face.

'Yesterday.'

'Was it bad?'

'Yes.'

He rubbed his temples. 'The house has gone.'

'Thank you for bringing Lilly. You can stay for a bit — I think you need to go back to sleep. I don't want Andarta after me.'

'You won't. She still hates me, but thanks.'

'She doesn't hate you, Laran...She just never really understood you properly and because of that, feels as though she can't trust you anymore,' Rose replied gently. 'I don't really know what happened there. To be honest, all the signs indicate you should be perfect for each other, but apparently it isn't meant to be. I'm sorry for that, I really am. But frankly, after what happened between you, her, and Holly, I can honestly say that I can see where she's coming from.' Rose smiled at him.

'I know, and I don't blame her. I can't seem to make it work out with anyone, can I? Maybe it's a punishment, and I am doomed to be forever alone?' Laran asked her, with such a look of dejection and misery that Rose couldn't help but to feel for him.

'Now, don't be like that. You're not being punished. You're not a bad person. You've made some mistakes in your past ... well, a lot of mistakes, but you've never intentionally hurt anyone you care about. I mean, come on, my daughter loved you, and it may have been the thing that got her killed, but she loved you none the less. Even then, I don't think it was entirely your fault, not directly at least; you just misunderstood the way she felt. Lilly seems to trust you, and she is probably right to. But know this, if you misplace that trust like you did my daughter's love, I might not be so forgiving this time. Anyway, what about Sophie? She loved you in her way.'

'How do you know about her? No one knows about that,' he replied, a look of shock and anger briefly showing on his face before being replaced by resignation. This was Rose, after all; he had never had any secrets from her.

'Laran, did you really think Lord Hurleston and I would

just let you disappear after Helen? Of course, we knew about her. She was your wife. Don't worry. No one else does. The twins are quite safe. I am glad you trusted Anahuit after Sophie died but you can't hide them forever,' Rose admonished gently.

Chapter Ten

I t took a few seconds for Lilly to remember where she was. She was in her old bedroom at Gran's. For a moment she stared up at the familiar ceiling rose and faded wall-paper, wondering why she wasn't at home. Then the acrid tang of smoke in her hair brought it all flooding back — the fire, the panic, William lying limp on the grass.

She shivered despite the central heating. After a long shower, she dug through the drawers and found some of her old clothes from when she was younger — a soft jumper, well-worn jeans — and padded downstairs barefoot.

Rose was in the kitchen, the radio murmuring in the background as she ironed a freshly laundered shirt. The faint scent of lavender starch mingled with toast.

'Feeling better?' Gran asked without looking up.

'Yes, thank you, Gran,' Lilly said, filling the kettle and glancing

over.

'David rang. Said William's fine, but they're keeping him in one more night to be sure. And Sarah called — Willow's perfectly fine, she can stay with her for as long as you need.'

Rose gave the shirt a sharp flick before pressing the hot iron down again.

'Is Laran still here?' Lilly asked.

'Yes. I sent him to bed. He'd only just woken up yesterday, you know — shouldn't have been gallivanting around the countryside after you,' Gran replied, a note of mild rebuke in her tone. 'Why don't you take him a coffee while I make him something to eat? He's going to need the calories to recover properly.'

Lilly made the coffee and carried it upstairs. The curtains were still drawn; the room was dim, smelling faintly of clean laundry and the earthy tang of rain from the open sash. Laran lay sprawled across the bed, the blanket tangled around his waist. She set the mug down quietly and crossed to the window to pull back the curtains.

The pale light flooded in — and she froze. It wasn't Laran's face she saw in that moment. It was William's.

The resemblance was so stark it winded her. The tilt of the jaw, the dark lashes against his skin, even the way one arm was crooked above his head. She sat down heavily on the edge of the bed, mind racing, barely aware that his eyes had opened and were watching her.

'Lilly, what's wrong?' His voice was rough from sleep. He reached for her hand. She blinked, shook herself. 'There's a coffee on the side.

Gran's ironed your shirt.' She rose quickly, before her voice could betray the confusion and anger roiling inside her.

Downstairs, she found Rose still at the ironing board. 'You knew, didn't you?' The words came out sharper than she'd intended.

'Yes, of course I knew.'

'And you never thought to tell me? You never thought that I might need to know?' Lilly asked.

'No, not really. It's not as if this information changes anything.'

'What? This changes everything. William is Laran's son. Do you even know what that might mean for him?'

'No, frankly I don't. But when Helen died, Lord Hurleston and I decided he would be far better off with you and David in a loving functional family than with Laran. He was in no state to take care of a child. He was heartbroken.

You have to understand, they aren't like us Lilly, we had no way of knowing how he would behave, and I felt William would be safer with you. Frankly, I still stand by that decision,' Gran explained calmly, as Lilly paced the kitchen fuming. 'We had two traumatised little boys. We had to consider their well-being above everything else. Andarta stepped in and took Gaillardia, as he was all elf. We couldn't expect her to take William. David was the logical choice.'

Rose gathered her handbag and car keys.

'But throughout all of it, you never once thought to tell me any of this?' Lilly responded angrily.

'No. Would it have changed the way you behaved? Would you have raised William any differently? Loved him any differently? You gave him a normal life, a normal upbringing, and that is exactly what he needed. Not to mention what Helen would have wanted. Now, I can see you're upset, and you probably want to discuss this some more with Laran. I've said my piece, and you can think what you like of me, but go easy on him. He didn't know it was all our doing.'

With that, Gran picked up her coat and walked out. Lilly watched Gran drive away and then went back to the kitchen. Althea and Tammy were at the table eating toast.

Lilly made Laran an omelette. The activity helped to calm her down as she waited for him to come downstairs.

'Lilly, are you all right?' Asked Althea.

'Yes, Althea. Could you two make yourselves scarce for a little while? I need to talk to Laran alone.'

'Of course. We'll go back outside.' Both elves got up and went back out into the garden, just as Laran came down- stairs. Lilly placed the omelette on the table. 'Gran says you need to eat lots. Do you want another coffee?' Lilly asked, noticing the red scar on his side as she reached for his shirt.

'Thank you, Lilly,' he could sense something was wrong, but just assumed that she was still put out by her house burning down.

'I know, Laran,' she said, watching him eat. He met her gaze, then pushed the plate away and took a long sip of coffee. 'You're Simon,' she added, voice firm.

'Did Andarta finally tell you? I knew she was annoyed, but this is low — even for her.'

'No. It was just now, when you were sleeping. You look exactly like William.'

He tried for a half-smile. 'Well, my hair was different back then...'

'That doesn't even make sense,' she snapped. 'Why didn't you say something? All that time at the castle, and you kept it to your- self. And David — loving, trusting David — stepped in and raised your son, buried your wife. We thought you were dead.'

Laran stared into his coffee. 'I can't ever repay what he's done for me. But after Helen died... I couldn't face him. Too much damage had been done.'

'Then tell me about it,' Lilly said, more quietly now. 'You owe me that much.' In the still warmth of Rose's kitchen, with the rain ticking softly against the window, he told her everything — Holly's death, the guilt, the slow unravelling of himself. How he'd reinvented himself as Simon Penatome, met David at university, fallen for Helen. The birth of William. The night the

Dark Elves came, and how he'd woken days later on a riverbank, believing them both gone.

How he'd gone back to Andarta for Gail's sake. How years later, in the halls of FERA, he'd seen William alive — holding David's hand — and nearly broken apart. How Hurleston had locked him in his office until Andarta arrived, and how she'd convinced him to let William stay in the human world.

By the time he fell silent, Lilly's fury had ebbed into a quiet, aching pity. She reached for his hands. 'I'm so sorry.'

'Who else knows?' she asked after a moment.

'Until recently, just Andarta, Rose, and Hurleston. This summer, Hyperion worked it out. And Gail... he realised in the castle. Asked me a couple of days ago. I brushed him off.'

'Yes. He's your image,' Lilly said softly. 'Though David says he's got Helen's smile.'

Laran gave a wry smile — and then a voice came from the doorway.

'Mum?'

Both turned to see Willow, pale and tear-streaked, standing there. Her eyes darted between them, unreadable. Then she turned and bolted before Lilly could move.

'Willow, wait! This isn't what it seems!' Lilly called, hurrying after her.

Chapter Eleven

The garden gate clicked behind her as Willow bolted across the yard. The air still held a ghost of smoke — not the sharp bite of flames, but that clingy, grey smell that got everywhere. Jacen was halfway to the barn when she reached him, and without thinking she threw herself into his arms. He staggered back a step, catching her before they both toppled into the mud.

'You okay?' he asked, holding her at arm's length to see her face.

'No. First the fire...' Her voice cracked. 'We had to climb out the landing window. Downstairs was an inferno and Mum couldn't put it out. And then—' She swallowed. 'William... he stopped breathing. Dad was doing CPR. I thought—' The rest jammed in her throat.

Jacen's arms tightened round her. 'That's a lot for one night.'

She nodded against his shoulder, managed a shaky breath, then scrunched her nose. 'Also, you smell like cows.'

He huffed a laugh. 'And you smell like a campfire that lost.'

'Wow. Thanks.' She pulled away, but the corner of her mouth twitched.

'It's just the smoke!' he called after her as she stomped towards the house.

A hot shower later, Willow felt almost human. Watching the soot spiral down the drain had been oddly satisfying, like rinsing the night out of her skin. She padded back in borrowed pyjamas, rubbing her hair with a towel.

'Where's Heli?' Jacen asked from his bed.

'Gone to Gran Rose's with Althea — elf training week.' Willow dropped beside him and tugged the duvet over her knees.

He hesitated. 'You going to tell me what happened before the fire?'

She stared at her hands. 'We went after Gail and William. Proper rescue — Mum dropped a storm on the moor, rangers on horseback... I rode with Lord Aquillo. It worked, but it was close.'

Her throat tightened again. 'They're linked, Jay. If something happens to William, Gail feels it. When William went down last night...' She trailed off, the thought snagging — Canada felt very far away.

Jacen's brows drew together. 'Are they okay now?'

'William's in hospital overnight. Mum says he'll be fine.' She didn't add the rest — that she kept imagining Gail crumpling half a world away. Not yet.

'So... Gail,' he said, raising an eyebrow. 'What's he like?'

She smiled faintly. 'Funny. Brave.'

'Sounds like a good bloke.'

'He is. I just hope he's all right. He's in Canada with his mum

now.'

Sarah cracked the door. 'Lights out, you two.'

'Night, Mum,' Jacen said. They both tried not to laugh until the door clicked shut.

Willow woke to bacon and an empty bed. Nicola breezed in with a bundle of clothes.

'These should fit. Jacen's helping Dad finish the milking,' she said, dumping the pile on the chair.

'Thanks,' Willow managed, and smiled. She ate in the garden, the morning bright but thin, that washed-out light you got after rain. Jacen was still scraping the yard with the tractor, the blade clanking softly. Her phone buzzed in her pocket.

10.31, Willow:

How are you really? Mum said what happened when William stopped breathing.

10.32, Gail:

I'm okay now. Scared everyone though, apparently.

Still not used to whatever this link is.

I'm fine — just tired of everyone fussing.

10.33, Willow:

It scared me too.

Our house burnt down. William's in hospital overnight but

they say he'll be okay.

10.34, Gail:

Wish I could be there.

. . .

10.34, Willow:
Me too. Gotta go, txt later x

'Ready, then?' Jacen called, hopping down from the tractor and wiping his hands on his jeans.

'Yeah. Your mum said we should be back for lunch,' Willow replied, tucking her phone away.

They took the lane side by side. The hedges dripped, beaded with last night's rain. When they reached the top of the drive, the smell of wet ash rose to meet them.

'Ready?' he asked.

She nodded, jaw tight. He squeezed her hand — and yelped, jerking back as a sharp jolt snapped between them.

'Ow! Willow, what was that?'

'I didn't—' She reached for him again on instinct. A blue arc jumped from her fingers to his; the crack made them both flinch. Jacen went down on his backside in the gravel.

'I'm sorry! I'm so sorry—'

'Don't touch me!' He shuffled away, startled anger flashing and then fading as he saw her face. 'What on earth was that?'

'I don't know. It's never happened before.' Mortification burned in her cheeks. 'I'm sorry, Jay.'

He blew out a breath. 'Since when can you electrocute people? Or is this a new thing you thought you'd test on me first?'

'It's not—' Her voice wobbled. 'I'm sorry.' And before he could say anything else, she turned, pressed her palm to the oak at the edge of the drive, and stepped into its shimmer.

'Willow, wait!' he called, scrambling to his feet. But the bark had already sealed, the air stilling as if nothing had happened.

Willow stepped out into Gran's garden. She scrubbed at her eyes with her sleeve, drew a breath, and went round to the back door. The kitchen was warm, the radio murmuring, and for a second it felt like everything might be normal.

Then she saw her mum in Laran's arms. Something in her chest lurched. It was too much — the fire, the moor, William, the way the world had tilted in the space of a night. She backed out, heart thudding, and fled to the beech at the end of the lawn. Her palm hit the cool bark; the green-gold light flared.

She stepped into a different wood — tall trunks, damp leaf mould under her knees, the air green and quiet. Willow sank down and finally let herself cry.

Chapter Twelve

Gail was lying on the sofa in the living room with his EarPods in, listening to his favourite band while reading a book on his laptop. His plaster-cast wrist rested awkwardly across his stomach, the white bandage stark against his dark T-shirt. Andarta had gone back to her library. He was bored and really wanted to go outside or do some sort of exercise, but his lungs still hurt from the smoke. Because of that, the nurse had banned him from anything strenuous for at least the next twenty-four hours.

Being linked to William really sucked, he decided, and wished they could have linked him to someone a bit more careful. The memory of yesterday — that crushing pain in his chest, the sudden fight for air when William had collapsed in the fire — still sat raw in his mind. Even now, if he thought about it too hard, he could feel the echo of that panic.

He'd texted Willow earlier and she'd said she would message him later. He guessed their date had been cancelled again. He sighed, feeling disappointed.

A sudden flash of light caught his eye. Thinking Laran was back, he struggled to his feet, careful not to jar his wrist, and went to let him in — but when he opened the door, there was no sign of Laran. Instead, Willow was sitting on the ground by the tree, crying.

'Willow? What are you doing here?' he asked, walking towards her.

'Stay back — don't come near me. I might hurt you,' she sobbed. Gail knelt in front of her, his casted hand resting gently on her knee while his good hand reached for hers. 'How are you going to do that?' he asked softly, feeling a faint tingle run up his arm. He frowned. 'Why don't you come inside and explain?'

Once inside, Willow watched as Gail opened a dark wooden cupboard with his good hand, fetched a glass, and filled it with ice-cold water from the fridge. He handed it to her, careful not to bump his plaster against the counter.

'So, what brings you here, apart from the fact you obviously couldn't wait to see me?' Gail grinned, pleased when Willow managed a grin back.

'Well, obviously,' she said in an exaggerated voice. 'I couldn't keep away, so I devised this plan to electrocute my best friend.'

'Wow, that sucks. I bet she was mad?'

'He,' Willow corrected. 'I electrocuted Jacen. Yeah, he was.' Her eyes shone with unshed tears.

'How?' Gail asked, frowning. Despite never having met Jacen, he felt a stab of jealousy.

'With my hands. All this electricity just came out of my fingers and knocked him off his feet. So, I touched a tree and ended up here. I'm not sure why.'

'You're not sure why? I thought we'd already established you were drawn to my magnetic personality,' Gail replied with a deadpan look.

'Oh yeah, sorry,' Willow giggled.

'Well, at least it was Jacen and not William. I'm not sure I could cope with that.'

'Ha — must suck being linked to him, huh?'

'It has its moments.' Gail gave her a pointed look. 'Especially when his house catches fire and he stops breathing. I'm not keen on repeating that one.'

Willow's smile faded. 'I was there. I saw him lying on the grass. I was terrified for him — and you. Mum told me what was happening to you in Canada. I kept thinking... if we lost him, we'd lose you too.'

His expression softened. 'Well, I'm still here. And he's okay. But... yeah. It was close.'

'It scared me,' Willow admitted quietly.

'It scared me too,' he said, then nodded toward her hands.

'Now — show me these amazing lightning hands of yours.'

Willow set her hands on the table. Gail took them in his good hand and the awkward crook of his cast, turning them over and inspecting them. 'They look pretty normal to me,' he concluded with a smile.

'Thank you, Doctor Gail.' Willow giggled, enjoying the fact he was still holding her hands. She pulled one free and casually touched the glass — ice crystals spread instantly. She looked up at

Gail, raising a brow. 'Not so ordinary.'

'Amazing.' He chuckled, tipping the glass until a perfect block of ice slid onto the table. Putting the glass down, he took her hands again, holding her gaze.

'That was pretty cool,' Gail said, failing to keep a straight face.

'Good grief,' Willow sighed. 'Jacen cracked that joke last night when I froze his drink.'

'You were with him last night?'

'Well, yeah — where else was I going to sleep? My house burnt down,' she said dryly.

'Oh. Right. Good point,' Gail said, catching the way her eyes filled with tears again. 'What else can you do?'

'Not much. Nothing as dramatic as that,' she chuckled. 'Can't wait to get the weather.'

'I think I can,' Gail laughed, relieved when Willow joined in.

'I think Jacen would agree with you on that one. He's so patient with me. I hate that I hurt him.'

'I'm sure he'll forgive you. He sounds like a good friend.'

'Yeah, he is.'

Hearing voices, Andarta walked in to see who Gail was talking to. She stopped, slightly taken aback to find Willow there and more so to see them holding hands and laughing together.

'Hello, Willow. What are you doing here? Is Lilly here?'

Andarta glanced around, expecting to see Lilly. When she realised she wasn't there, she turned back to Willow, noting her puffy eyes and tear-marked face.

'Oh! Willow had an accident,' Gail explained, his cast still resting on the table as her fingers curled lightly over it.

'Oh dear, do tell. Did you freeze something again?'

'No, not this time. Don't worry. It was nothing serious. Anyway, I'd better go. Everyone will be looking for me and I don't want to intrude.' Even though she found Gail's mum a bit intimidating, she would have liked to stay longer.

'You're not intruding, Willow. Is she, Mum?' Gail asked, disappointed she was leaving.

'You're more than welcome to stay if you like. Poor Gail could use the company.'

'I'd love to stay, if that's alright with you?' Willow replied, sitting back down and taking Gail's good hand in hers again.

'Alright then. I'll phone Lilly and arrange it.' Andarta left, and the two of them grinned at each other like a pair of idiots.

'Going to show me round, then?' Willow asked.

'Um, yeah, if you like.' Gail got up, balancing the weight on his good hand, and led her into the living room.

Willow looked around and walked over to the grand piano that dominated the space. 'Do you play?' she asked, as she studied the family photos on top — many of Gail as a boy, though none from babyhood.

'Err, yeah, I do,' he said, sitting down and adjusting his cast slightly before starting to play a simple tune. Willow recognised it and smiled. She shuffled next to him and played alongside him. Gail grinned and shifted into something trickier to see if she could keep up. Willow giggled and followed, making him laugh.

'How long have you been playing?' he asked.

'Five years. You didn't expect that, did you?' Willow's grin was mischievous.

'No, I didn't,' Gail confessed.

'Where's your room, then?' she asked, blinking when he smiled at her.

'Upstairs. I can show you.' Gail stood, catching her hand in his good one, and led her upstairs.

Willow smiled as they entered. The wallpaper was covered with aeroplanes; model planes hung from the ceiling. A desk by the window displayed photos of Gail and Laran next to a helicopter, and another of Gail on a plane. Fossils sat to one side.

Shelves on another wall held a remote-control helicopter and books about flying.

'I haven't really changed it since I was ten,' he explained, slightly embarrassed. 'I was away, first at boarding school, then university, so there seemed little point. Besides, I like it.'

'It's... er... very boyish,' she teased, making him chuckle.

'Uh huh.' He tried not to laugh, looking into her cloudy grey eyes. Slowly, he leaned in and kissed her, careful with the arm in plaster as his good hand cupped her cheek.

Willow kissed him back, her hands resting lightly on his arms so she wouldn't knock the cast. She'd never been kissed like this before — not even by Jacen. Finally, she pulled away, a little breathless.

'That was amazing,' she breathed.

'Hmm.' Gail let go of her, straightening his shirt one-handed.

'So, you are an elf,' Willow said with a sly smile.

'Um, yes,' he replied, voice hesitant.

She reached up, running her fingers through his hair until his ears were exposed. He hissed softly, his cheeks flushing.

'That... that is quite rude,' he breathed.

'Really?' Willow asked, studying the slightly elongated ear before sitting back. 'Are you sure you're an elf?'

'Yes, Willow — and they are very sensitive.'

'Just thought they'd be... more,' she shrugged, making him laugh.

'We adapted to fit in with the humans. So, you aren't going to freeze the house?'

'Oh no, I have that under control,' she said, glancing away.

'Sorry I missed our date.'

'Yeah, I was disappointed, but I'm happy to do this instead,'

Gail grinned, pulling her against him carefully, so as not to bump her with the cast, and kissed her again.

'Hmm,' Willow managed, her stomach flipping as the connection between them deepened.

'Mm, Willow,' Gail murmured as her hands slipped under his shirt against his warm skin. The surge of nature made his connection to nature — and to her — flare. He shifted, his casted wrist resting awkwardly against the bedspread, but he didn't care.

Suddenly, Gail remembered where they were. Letting go, he sat up. 'Sorry.'

'Yeah,' Willow said, straightening her blouse.

'Is this you?' she asked, picking up a photo from his bedside table — a man and woman holding a baby. The edges were ragged, slightly burnt.

'Yes. My birth parents,' he said quietly, taking it back.

'Oh.' The silence stretched before she changed the subject.

'You like flying, then? It was so cool when you flew us home.'

'Yeah, I've been wanting to fly Taranis' helicopter for ages,' he said with a dazzling smile that made her stomach somersault. She reached up and kissed him again, his good arm wrapping around her as the plastered one rested against her side.

Now that, she thought, was a proper kiss.

Chapter Thirteen

Lilly had run out after Willow, but Willow touched the tree before she could stop her. One blink, and she was gone. Lilly stood there for a moment, breathing hard, wondering why her daughter had even been here in this state.

She pulled her phone from her pocket and called Sarah.

'Hi Sarah, it's Lilly. Is Jacen okay? Willow's upset about some- thing and she was with him last. Has he said anything?'

'No, I think they had some sort of falling out. He got back five minutes ago and went straight to his room, slammed the door.

You know what teenagers are like. I'll give him a few minutes to cool off and then interrogate him, if you like. They'll probably be best friends again by tomorrow.'

'Okay, thanks, Sarah. You take care. Bye.'

The moment she hung up, her phone rang again. To her surprise, it was Andarta.

'Hello?'

'Hi, Lilly — it's Andarta.'

'Oh, hello. How are you?'

'I'm fine, thank you. Listen... I don't know if you know, but we've got Willow here. She seemed upset, and we said she could stay if she wanted. You don't mind, do you?'

'Wait — stay where? At the flat?'

'No, she came to our house... in Canada.'

'Canada... wow. Okay. Did she say what was wrong?'

'Not really. But from what I gather, she hurt her friend Jacen — electrocuted him, according to Gail. He's with her now in the kitchen — still looking a bit pale after what happened the other day, but fussing over her all the same.'

Lilly's chest tightened. She still remembered the call. William fighting for breath, Gail collapsing thousands of miles away, both boys tangled in that dangerous bond.

'Right. I'm with Laran — we'll be there shortly. Bye.' She turned to Laran.

'Um, Willow is at your house.'

'I'm not going to get snow in my kitchen, am I?' Laran asked, frowning.

'You heard about that?'

'Yeah. Gail mentioned it.'

'Well, let's see, shall we — although I can't promise anything,' Lilly said with a small smile, taking his hand.

'Lilly, lovely to see you,' Andarta greeted warmly when they arrived, then turned to Laran. 'Darling, you look terrible. You should go back to bed. I'll send Gail to fetch you for dinner.'

'Erm, yeah... sure,' Laran said, edging past her suspiciously and disappearing into the house, leaving Lilly on the doorstep.

'Would you like tea or coffee?' Andarta asked.

'Tea, please.' Somewhere in the house, Lilly could hear muffled music, the low hum of voices, and a burst of laughter that made her think of Willow when she was very small.

'What happened?' she asked as Andarta set two mugs of tea on the table.

'From what I gather, she electrocuted her friend Jacen,' Andarta replied, smiling faintly.

'Oh yes, I can see why that upset her. Did she say how?'

'With her hands, apparently.'

Lilly considered this. 'She seems to be gaining her powers early. I mean, I couldn't do anything like that until my late teens, early twenties. She can already hear animals — that took me years. David had an incident with her in the greenhouses a couple of weeks ago too. I think she's starting to influence plants. And now she's here. That takes finesse and power.'

She sipped her tea. 'And of course, we had the incident at school... and then at the castle.'

'Ah yes, Gail told me all about it. Quite the adventure with your children again. How is William?'

'He's fine. David is with him.' Lilly paused, remembering again how Gail's breathing had faltered in Canada the moment William collapsed by the burning house.

Something in Lilly's openness softened Andarta's guarded manner. Perhaps Lilly wasn't so bad — even if she did look far too much like Holly. Maybe, in time, she could tolerate her.

'I could do some research,' Andarta offered. 'See if you should be concerned. I think Lord Hurleston still has records of all the past Mother Natures. He gave up trying to stop me snooping through FERA's archives years ago.'

'Thank you, Andarta. That would be useful.'

'So... what went on between you and Laran?' Andarta tried to sound casual, though a flicker of jealousy threaded her words.

'I found out about William.'

That wasn't the answer Andarta expected. 'How? Did he just tell you?'

'Of course not. That man is the most difficult person I've ever met. He infuriates me with all his secrets.'

Andarta laughed. 'Try living with him.'

'Joking aside, this is serious — for your boy and mine. Hyperion knows. He worked it out just by seeing Laran and William together. They look so alike. I can't believe I didn't see it sooner.

Even Gail noticed. How long before others do? And what else has William inherited from Laran? No one else knows about the link, but I'm worried for his safety.'

'Why not leave Willow here with us? I can take her shopping and she can keep Gail company. I'll do some research for you.

There have been other children — King Spring has had several over the years. This way you can deal with the house and FERA without worrying. Heli can visit as well, I'm sure Willow misses her. And for now, I think William's safe — until this summer he'd hardly met Laran or other elves, and it's seeing them together that makes people notice.'

'Thank you, Andarta. That would be great. And thank you for inviting Heli, but she's in training.'

'What would be great, Mum?' Willow's voice came from the doorway as she and Gail wandered in, holding hands. He still looked a little wan, his arm in plaster, but the colour in his face was better than Lilly expected.

'Andarta suggested you stay here for a while so I can sort work things out and find us somewhere to live.'

'I don't have any stuff, though. Everything burnt. And I was going to Jake's party tomorrow with Jacen — I missed the last one because I kept freezing stuff,' Willow grumbled.

'Well, you can't do that. It's best if you stay here tonight.'

'I suppose I can text Jacen and Jane,' Willow said reluctantly.

'Andarta will take you shopping. And if you're here, I know you're safe. I'm sure Gail can keep you entertained — and will understand if you electrocute him. Won't you, Gail?' Lilly teased.

Gail blushed, and Lilly hid a smile, wondering if his poor lungs had survived one fire only to be put at risk in an entirely different way.

'That's not funny, Mum,' Willow said, glaring.

Chapter Fourteen

Laran and Gail were sitting in the living room watching ice hockey and drinking beer. Of all the human sports, ice hockey seemed to resonate the most with Laran's more savage side. Gail, for his part, just enjoyed being with his father.

Neither of them paid Willow much attention as she walked in and plonked herself down on the sofa next to Laran. In fact, Gail hadn't paid her much attention at all since his dad had come home, and he hadn't tried to kiss her again.

'What are you watching?' she asked nonchalantly.

'NHL — Vancouver Canucks vs. the San Jose Sharks,' Laran replied, eyes still focused on the game.

'Oh, cool. Mind if I join you?' Willow asked, a little tentatively. She sometimes got the impression they forgot she was even there.

'Yeah, sure,' Laran said.

'Do you mind turning it up a little?' Willow asked again.

'Oh, right — the remote's right next to you on the coffee table.'

Willow picked it up and thumbed the volume button.

Nothing happened. She waved it through the air, still nothing. 'I think the remote's broken.'

'Oh, really? Well, there are some buttons on the side. Hang on,

I'll do it,' Gail said, smiling as he began to get up.

'It's fine. I've got it,' Willow replied, springing to her feet.

Laran, meanwhile, was inspecting the remote when black smoke began to curl from it.

'Willow, wait!' he shouted, suddenly figuring it out — but by then it was already too late.

'What is it?' Willow asked, turning back to Laran just as she went to press the side button on the television.

She yelped and leapt back. A plume of acrid smoke poured from the television and the screen went black.

'Never mind,' was all Laran said. Willow stood in silence for a minute as the blood rushed to her face.

'Oh my gosh. I'm so sorry,' she said, tears welling behind her eyes.

Sensing her upset, Laran stood to comfort her. 'Hey, don't worry about it. It was a rubbish game anyway, and I can always buy a new telly.' He smiled, stepping forward to hug her.

Only as he closed his arms around her did he realise it was probably a terrible idea — too late. Something hurled him across the room, crashing into the sofa and tipping it over.

Laran came to a few seconds later to find Gail standing over him, looking worried. His head rang, vision blurry; he'd somehow ended up sprawled in a heap behind the sofa.

Grunting, he dragged himself to his feet. 'Where's Willow?' he asked, scanning the room.

'She ran off. I think she was pretty upset,' Gail said.

'And you're still here. Why?'

'What?' Gail asked, confused. 'I wanted to see if you were alright.'

'Why the heck didn't you go after her? Don't worry about an old duffer like me — now go, GO!' Laran ordered, trying to block out the pain in his head.

'Oh. Right.' Gail rushed from the room.

'It'll take more than a sixteen-year-old girl to take me out,' Laran muttered, heading into the kitchen for a bag of frozen peas.

Andarta had just come back from a long walk in the surrounding pine forest and was looking forward to settling down in her library with a good book. Entering the brightly lit room, she noticed Willow sitting at the farthest table, head in her hands. She looked like she was crying.

'Hey, hey — what's the matter?' Andarta asked, walking over.

'Don't come near me. Just... stay away!' Willow said, looking up.

'Okay — but only if you explain why you're crying. How about that?' Andarta replied, puzzled and a little concerned.

'I'm a murderer. Just stay away!' Willow sobbed.

'Really? Who did you kill?' Andarta asked, intrigued despite herself.

'I... I killed Laran!' she wailed, crying harder.

'What? No, you didn't. I just saw him in the kitchen.'

'What?' Willow's tears slowed a little.

'He's in there with an ice pack on his head. I'm guessing that's because of you. Why don't you tell me what happened?'

'We... we were watching telly, and I tried to turn up the

volume, but the telly broke. I thought it was my fault and got upset, so Laran came over to comfort me — and that's when I thought I'd accidentally killed him,' Willow said between sniffles.

'Ah, sweetie, you didn't kill him, bless you. You just bashed him about a bit. He's fine — probably laughing about it with Gail right now,' Andarta said gently.

'What am I going to do? I can't go around electrocuting people for the rest of my life, can I?'

'Well, no. But luckily for you, I've been doing research — and I think I may have found a solution,' Andarta said, pleased with herself.

'Well? What is it?' Willow asked, wiping her eyes.

'For some reason, an electrical potential is building up in your body. It discharges whenever you touch something conductive — like Laran.'

Willow laughed despite herself. 'So, how do we fix it?'

'I'm not sure. But I think we can make you harmless for short periods by discharging the current through a conductor. It's not perfect, but until you learn control, it's the best we've got.

Earthing yourself through your feet is risky — it could burn you, and I'm rather attached to my cream carpet.'

She crossed to a bookcase, pulling out an old map. 'I've found a suitable alternative — a disused radio mast nearby. And I thought the walk might be nice for you and Gail, especially now the television's broken.'

Late afternoon, Willow and Gail were walking along a dirt track toward the mast. Gail was in the lead, keeping a cautious distance from her. His breathing wasn't quite even — a leftover from William's recent respiratory arrest — and Willow noticed him subtly rubbing his chest every so often.

They reached the mast and stared up at it.

'What now?' Willow asked.

'I guess you just... walk up and touch it,' Gail said.

'Right.' She squeezed through a hole in the rusted fence, walked up to the base, and placed her hand on the metal.

Nothing happened.

'Did it work?' Gail called from outside.

'I think so... but I didn't feel anything.'

Gail joined her inside the fence and reached for her hand. Nothing.

'I guess it worked then. That was anti-climactic,' Willow said.

'Not for me,' Gail muttered, looking relieved.

They walked back in silence, but it wasn't comfortable silence. Willow wondered if he was avoiding her on purpose. Maybe he regretted their kiss. She thought about Jacen — who was never shy about his feelings.

Gail was equally tangled in thought. What if she thought he'd been too forward? What if she didn't want him to kiss her again?

He hated how his chest still felt tight from the fire — it made him seem weak.

'Um, we could go to that party now,' Gail suggested.

'What, Jake's? We missed it.'

'Oh.' He lapsed into silence again.

'Thanks for the thought,' Willow said softly, slipping her hand into his. He smiled but still didn't speak, his mind racing. She's holding my hand... what do I say?

Willow bit her lip. Enough was enough. A minute later she added, 'Gail, are you telepathic with anyone else? Or is that just a special William thing?'

'Mostly William,' he said, eyes forward. 'Brought up human. You learn to keep your head quiet.'

'Mmm.' She shot him a sideways look. 'Don't turn round, but we're being followed.'

'By what?' he asked sharply.

'A bear. Just beyond those trees. Been there a while.'

'I think we should walk faster — then run for the house,' Gail said, lengthening his stride, which made him slightly breathless.

'No, wait — let me try something first. If it doesn't work, we run.'

'Willow, I don't think we should mess about with a bear.'

'What have we got to lose?'

'Fine. But if it goes wrong, I'm making sure it eats you first,' he teased weakly.

Willow smirked. 'Hardly gentlemanly.' She put her hands on either side of his head. 'Relax.'

Gail rolled his eyes but let her in.

She reached for the bear's mind. It stopped, sensing her.

'Hello, Child of Nature,' the bear said.

'Hello. We're just walking — nice woods you have.'

'I was thinking about eating you,' the bear said bluntly.

Gail's eyes went wide.

'Not a good idea,' Willow said firmly. 'Mother Nature would be cross.'

'He's not a Child of Nature,' the bear said, turning its gaze to Gail.

'Run,' Gail said, grabbing Willow's arm.

'Yeah, good plan.'

They sprinted, Gail's breath rasping in his chest as the bear charged. He vaulted the garden gate, landing in a roll before opening it for Willow. The bear roared, then eventually wandered off.

'Goodbye, Mister Bear,' Willow giggled.

'I wasn't really going to eat him,' the bear grumbled.

'I know that. But he didn't.'

'King Autumn would be cross if I ate Lord Aristata. See you around, Child of Nature.'

'That was brilliant. I've never talked to a bear before,' Willow gasped, still catching her breath.

'Brilliant?! Are you mental? He was going to eat us, and you think it's funny,' Gail shot back, his arms folded tight, his whole posture radiating disbelief.

Willow grinned up at him. 'Yeah, didn't expect that. I thought he'd want to be my friend.'

'Willow, why would a bear want to be your friend? You're in his food chain sweet spot.'

'Maybe I just have a way with animals,' she teased, stepping closer.

'Or maybe you're reckless,' Gail countered, but there was the tiniest twitch of a smile at the corner of his mouth.

'Come on, Gail. You didn't really think he was going to eat us, did you?' she said, tilting her head, her cloudy-grey eyes locking with his.

He tried to hold his ground, but she'd already closed the space between them, her confidence quiet but sure. 'Look, I'm sorry. I promise — no more befriending dangerous predators. Unless they're cute.'

That earned her a reluctant laugh.

Willow's smile softened. 'And for the record, I still like me. Even with the whole "more than human" thing.'

Before Gail could answer, she stood on tiptoe and kissed

him. Not a nervous brush, but slow, certain, her hands light against his chest.

He hesitated for a heartbeat, then slid his good arm around her waist, drawing her in.

'Apology accepted,' he murmured, his voice low.

'Good. I'd have been disappointed if you said no,' she said against his mouth, her tone teasing but her eyes warm.

Gail's lips quirked. 'Guess I'd better keep saying yes then.'

'Guess you should,' she replied, kissing him again — and this time, he met her halfway.

'Good.' She let the moment rest, then: 'Gail... who is Lord Aristata?'

He went still. 'Where did you hear that?'

'The bear said it.'

'He's no one. He's dead.' He looked away.

'Oh.' She kept her voice light, though a small knot tightened in her stomach. 'It's not you, then?'

'Nope. Not me,' he said quietly, then kissed her again as if to move the conversation along. Willow kissed him back, but tucked the answer away. He was lying. She didn't know why — yet — but she wasn't going to push it. Not now.

They walked the rest of the way to the house hand in hand, trading small jokes, letting the adrenaline ebb. At the gate she nudged his shoulder with hers.

'You're very brave for someone who apparently nearly got eaten,' she said.

'You're very impossible for someone who apparently befriends bears,' he replied, and that time she laughed so hard she had to lean into him. He caught her easily, careful as ever, and didn't let go until her laughter faded to a smile.

Chapter Fifteen

'Annie, where are you?' Laran called as he walked down the hall toward the kitchen.

'In the kitchen,' she replied.

'What are you doing?'

'Sending emails to Lord Hurleston. Trying to get more information on Willow's condition. Also, you owe me ten dollars.'

'What? Why?' 'See for yourself.' She grinned, grabbing his arm and tugging him toward the window.

Outside, Willow was in the garden with Gail. He was leaning back against the bench, one arm in plaster, still moving a little stiffly when he laughed. Willow stepped closer, her smile mischievous, and without hesitation reached up to kiss him — not a shy peck, but certain and unhurried, her hands resting lightly on his shoulders as if she'd been doing this for years.

Gail blinked in surprise, then grinned into the kiss and let her pull him closer.

'Oh man. She kissed him first?' Laran muttered.

'Yep.'

'Damn.' He watched them for another second — Willow

laughing softly at something Gail murmured, brushing her fingers through his hair like she'd decided she had the right to — before glancing at Andarta. 'You know what this means, don't you?'

'Yeah — teenagers in love. I'll be hiding in my library if you need me.' She turned to leave, throwing over her shoulder, 'I fancy your chicken chasseur if you're cooking.' Her purposeful sway made him chuckle despite himself.

Laran thought he'd preferred Willow when she was electrocuting people — at least then she wasn't glued to his son. No matter what room he went in, they were there, kissing.

After the bear incident, he'd gone into town and bought along metal pole and some rope. With Andarta and Gail's help, they'd set it in the garden so Willow didn't have to walk miles to earth herself.

Unfortunately, it freed up more time for her to kiss Gail. Andarta wasn't helping either; she'd retreated to her library, smirking every time she caught Laran glaring. After a couple more days of stumbling across the pair mid-snog, Laran barricaded himself in his study.

Checking his emails, he found five updates from Hàlfr about dark elf movements, and — more unexpectedly — a message from Taranis. The first paragraph was an overlong apology about the castle. Laran skipped it. The rest detailed Taranis's plans for setting up his own office at FERA, offering troops in exchange for a good word with Lilly and Hurleston.

Laran doubted it would work, but he liked Taranis well

enough to agree to meet him Monday. He sent the reply, then leaned back, running a hand through his hair, wondering how he'd survive until then.

A quiet knock interrupted his thoughts.

'Dad, can I talk to you for a minute?' Gail slipped in, closing the door behind him. He moved more slowly than usual, careful with his plastered arm, and sat opposite.

'Yeah, sure. What's the problem?' Laran asked.

'Um... currently it's raining in my bedroom, the bathroom plants won't stop growing, and every time we go for a walk, a herd of deer follows us. Oh — and last night I think she was channelling autumn, because I slept way too deeply for that to be normal.' He chuckled, rubbing his chest where the smoke injury still ached on bad days. 'Mum's sorting it. But... that's not why I'm here.' Laran raised an eyebrow.

'Willow knows my name. My real name.' Laran stilled. 'How?'

'The bear she was talking to referred to me by my title.' Laran's lips twitched. 'She talked to a bear?'

'Yeah, Dad. This isn't funny — it wanted to eat me.' Despite himself, Gail laughed, which quickly turned into a cough.

'Personally,' Laran smirked, 'I think her knowing your name is the least of your problems if you're dating her. You're still safe. Just... maybe keep her away from more bears.'

'Gee, thanks,' Gail said dryly. 'Dad... I can't hide forever.'

'I know, Gail. But we wanted you to have a life, have fun, be normal, before you become who you were born to be.' Laran's voice softened. 'Be nineteen. Enjoy it. Let me do the worrying.'

Before Gail could reply, the lights cut out.

'Willow!' he called, just as they flickered back on.

'Fixed it!' Andarta shouted, giggling.

'Whoops, sorry!' Willow's voice followed, equally bright with laughter.

Laran looked at his son, who just shrugged — and then burst out laughing.

Chapter Sixteen

David was in Rose's kitchen, helping her prepare dinner, when there was a knock at the door. He answered it to find Detective Inspector Hepworth. David recognised him from the hospital after the fire — the detective had visited to inform him he would be overseeing the investigation into its cause.

'Oh, hello Inspector, how are you?' David asked politely.

'I'm well, thank you, Mr Milbank. May I come in?'

'Yes, yes, of course.' David led him through to the cluttered and cramped sitting room.

'How is the investigation going, Inspector? Do you know the cause of the fire?'

'Yes. The fire investigation team submitted their report to me yesterday. I've been through it, and it appears the fire was not an accident.' Hepworth leaned forward, clasping his hands.

'You mean someone started it on purpose?' David asked, shocked.

'It would appear so. The fire was started in the kitchen, and the forensic team found traces of an accelerant. Do you know of anyone who might hold a grudge against you, Mr Milbank?'

'No, not that I'm aware of,' David lied.

'Did you see anyone, or anything unusual, on the night of the fire?'

'No, not that I can recall.'

'Indeed. Well, here's my card and a copy of the report. I'll phone if anything else comes up.'

When the inspector left, David sat for a long while, turning over what he'd just heard. Why had he lied? On some level, he felt loyalty to Lilly — but he was certain it had been one of the elves she dealt with. Once again, her business was spilling into his personal life and endangering the people he cared about.

Anger simmered under his skin. He resolved to put his foot down before things turned into another Helen and Simon situation. He didn't know the details of their deaths, but the secrecy around it — and Rose and FERA's involvement — spoke volumes.

It was a long, dull Saturday afternoon, and Laran was bored. In fact, bored didn't quite cover it. He was on the front lawn, launching golf balls into the woods. Carefully placing his second- to-last ball on the turf, he readied himself for the swing of the century.

With a satisfying smack, the ball soared into the trees. Laran shaded his eyes, tracking it — until there was a loud thwack, followed by an indignant shout.

'Ow!'

Lilly emerged from the treeline, holding his golf ball and rubbing her head. She was in jeans and a sweater that flattered her figure, hair in a plait down her back, no make-up that he could see. The effect was disarmingly natural — and, if he was honest, extremely appealing.

'Laran, why on earth is it raining golf balls?' she demanded.

'Sorry, I was bored, and this was helping.'

'Well, it's a good job I arrived when I did. Who knows what hare-brained scheme you'd come up with once you ran out of balls?'

'Search the woods looking for them?' he suggested, the corner of his mouth twitching.

'Hmm, yes, I'd probably do the same.' She smiled. 'Anyway, I've brought you something better to do. Let's go to the safety of your study where we can talk in private.'

Laran's study was nothing like his sparse FERA office. A plush neutral carpet softened the floor, the tasteful décor complemented by a leather sofa and a large desk facing floor-to-ceiling windows over the garden and forest beyond. On the desk, framed photographs of Gail stood in pride of place.

'Where's Willow?' Lilly asked.

'Oh, I think she's kissing Gail somewhere. That all started after she accidentally set a bear on him.'

'What? How?'

'Apparently, she can talk to animals now. Thought she'd try it out on a bear they met in the woods — only the bear wanted to eat Gail.' Laran grinned.

Lilly was momentarily lost for words. 'Right... Well. This —'She passed him a large white envelope.

Laran opened it, scanned the contents. 'Arson, then,' he said, one eyebrow raised.

'It would appear so. It's getting personal, isn't it?'

'I presume you also suspect the Dark Elves?'

'Yes. I've been working with Hàlfr and Gail while you were recovering. We expected them to step up activity with you out of the way, but instead they went quiet — apart from the odd coach crash and unexplained murder. We think they're plan- ning some- thing big, and I don't mean burning my house down. There's something about it that nags at me. And then there's the attempt on Gail's life on the moor — Taranis is baffled.'

'Any idea what they're up to?'

'Hàlfr noticed something else. I've been tied up with natural disasters and a mess in Japan, so he's been going through the intel himself. There were Dark Elves at the castle helping Hyperion — but they're not his. The Emperor sent them. That's a direct viola- tion of the peace treaty. What if kidnapping the children was just the first step? What if the fire was part of it? We're harder to

protect if we're spread out.'

'Taranis mentioned something with Gail and William, but Gail didn't think they were Dark Elves. He thought they were Summer — and despite shooting him, he was sure they were there to kidnap him. They were very well informed.'

'FERA still isn't secure,' Lilly warned. 'What if the fire was aimed at William? What if someone knows? William said they knew who Gail was — as your sons. That they might have been after him as much as Gail.'

'That doesn't sound like paranoia,' Laran admitted. 'Gail mentioned the same — that it felt like a kidnap attempt on William too.'

'That doesn't worry you?'

'Of course it does. But Gail's had kidnap attempts before — he's the heir to Autumn Enterprises and one of the Council of

Sixteen. He's vulnerable in both worlds. I can arrange secu- rity for William if you want.'

'No. He's safe with David. But Laran — this thing with Gail and Willow. Should we allow it?'

'What? They're just kids. Why not?'

'Because if the Dark Elves want to hurt my children, going after Willow before she's fully trained would be easier. And her being with him could put him in more danger — after you've hidden him for so long.'

'We kept him hidden to give him a childhood. Many see him as a pawn. Elf aristocracy is not like the human world. We wanted him free from that until he's ready. I wouldn't risk him — or her.'

'I've read my mother's file. I know what happened, and I don't want my daughter dragged into danger by one of your games.'

'This isn't a game. Gail's the heir of the Third House of Autumn, son of Lord Aristata — my closest friend. There are still people who'd prefer he didn't live long enough to take his place. I wouldn't gamble with his life. Or hers.'

Lilly exhaled, some of the tension leaving her shoulders.

'Thank you. I just want all our children safe.'

'And they will be. Annie mentioned Willow's... abilities. I've seen them myself. I'll keep her safe, even from herself.'

At that moment, Willow walked in and hugged her mum.

'What's up, Gail?' Laran asked, noting his son's restless glance towards the windows.

'Someone's outside, hiding in the trees.'

'This can't be good. Come with me.'

Laran flicked a switch in his desk; the locks clicked into place and bomb-proof shutters slid over the windows. At the bookcase, he pressed a hidden button — the shelf swung back to reveal a staircase leading down.

'How long's this been here?' Gail asked, eyes wide.

'Since the house was built.'

'And what is it?' Willow asked, barely containing her excitement.

'My armoury. And under no circumstances are you to tell Andarta.'

'Understood,' Willow and Gail chorused. Lilly smirked.

Laran hit another switch, bathing the basement in light. Racks of weapons lined the walls — swords, sleek composite bows, pistols, gleaming assault rifles. Between them, mannequins stood in armour from across the ages: a shining medieval plate harness, a full set of samurai armour.

'Whoa,' Gail breathed, struggling not to let his jaw drop.

Chapter Seventeen

After a short train journey and a brisk walk, David, William and Andarta arrived at Kew Gardens. Damp air clung to their clothes, carrying the faint scent of wet earth and flowers. David flashed the man at the kiosk some sort of card, explaining they were there to see Dr Paul Kersey, Kew Gardens' lead botanist.

They met Dr Kersey outside the Palm House. William was left to explore while the botanist, David and Andarta discussed the strange plant growing back at the garden centre. Since the incident with Willow, it had completely overrun the greenhouse.

David had been unable to kill it — not that he'd really tried. As he suspected, it was a brand-new species, not yet classified. If Dr Kersey couldn't identify it either, David might be right.

That worried Andarta. The plant seemed to have an adverse effect on elves, and she'd already heard reports of it invading land and disrupting wildlife.

William didn't stray far. He climbed one of the spiral stair-cases in the Palm House to the second level, leaning on the cool iron rail to admire the thick canopy below. Warm, humid air rose from the dense leaves, beading his skin with moisture.

Twenty minutes later, David joined him, leaning beside him. Andarta followed, wearing a look of utter boredom.

'So, how'd it go?' William asked in sign language.

'Depends. Badly, because he has no idea what it is,' David signed back.

'And?' William raised an eyebrow.

'On the other hand, I've discovered a brand-new plant.

According to Willow, it's evil — but still brand new. I shall call it Trifidus Davida,' David said with mock grandeur. William laughed and shook his head. Andarta yawned, pretending to check her phone, but her eyes kept flicking up, clearly trying to follow their hands.

'I'm hungry,' William signed.

'You're always hungry. But so am I. Let's get the Tube back to London and find something to eat,' David said. William nodded.

They descended the staircase, the metal treads ringing under- foot, heading for the exit — and stopped. A tall, muscular bald man in a white T-shirt and jeans stepped into their path. Two more men flanked him.

David slowed. 'Excuse me, please?'

The man shook his head slowly, the sound of cricking neck joints carrying in the humid stillness. He clicked his knuckles, one by one.

'William, go the other way,' David ordered, turning — only to see three equally big men blocking the path behind.

'Gentlemen, we don't have any money and we don't want trouble. Let us by,' David tried.

They didn't answer. They just advanced, heavy boots thudding softly against the damp boards.

'Let me handle this,' Andarta said, stepping past him. She

glared up at the bald man. 'Listen, loser. My friend politely asked you to move and you ignored him. That's rude. I'm in a foul mood — jet-lagged, stuck on your disgusting underground system, and short on patience. Now, either you step aside, or I'm going to hurt you.'

They didn't step aside. Instead, they grimaced as if in pain.

Black hairs sprouted, skin turned dark blue, eyes glowed crimson.

Jagged teeth bared.

Dark elves.

'Give us the boy,' the leader rasped, his voice like gravel scraping metal.

'I don't think so,' David said, pushing William behind him.

'Will, buddy — in a minute, run. I'll distract them.'

The elves' clothes shimmered into leather armour. Most drew serrated black blades that caught the light like wet glass. The leader cracked his knuckles and lunged at Andarta.

She ducked, twisting behind him so fast the air stirred. In one move she vaulted onto his shoulders, her leg hooking under his arm, the other around his neck. She yanked backwards — the elf crashed to the ground with a bone-jarring thud. Before he could get up, she smashed his head into the floor, the sound a dull, final crack.

Another elf swung for her. She caught his wrist, bent it until his grip broke, caught the falling sword, and drove it into his stomach. He wheezed, folding around the blade.

David had his own problem. He scooped a fistful of damp soil from a raised bed, the scent of loam and crushed leaves filling his nose. The elf closed in — David flung the dirt into its eyes. It staggered, clawing at its face with a guttural snarl.

Another blade hissed through the air towards William — David shoved him clear.

'Run!' he barked.

William bolted into the dense greenery, fronds slapping his face, boots skidding on wet stone. He hoped the plants would slow his pursuer. They didn't.

He glanced back, tripped over a raised bed, and crashed to the path. Pain flared along his side. The elf laughed, flipped its sword into a reverse grip, and stabbed down — William rolled away and kicked it in the knee.

'For that, I'm going to make it hurt,' it snarled, tossing its sword aside.

It punched him hard in the chest, the impact knocking the breath from him in a rush. It yanked him up and kneed him in the stomach. William doubled over, gasping, before being slammed against a palm tree. Bark bit into the back of his head as fingers closed around his throat.

His vision darkened, sound muffling. Desperate, he went limp.

The elf dropped him and turned to look for its weapon.

William surged up and punched it in the head, his knuckles stinging.

Snarling, the elf stalked forward. William backed away until the tree stopped him. The blow to his head came hard — stars burst, and everything went black. The elf slung him over its shoulder, stepped into the shadows, and vanished.

Outside the Palm House, Andarta brushed herself down, surrounded by groaning, incapacitated elves. The air reeked of sweat, iron, and damp leaves.

'I think we handled that rather well,' she said brightly.

'Speak for yourself,' David muttered through the tissue pressed to his bleeding nose. He looked around. 'Where's William?'

'I thought he was with you!' Andarta scanned the area, spot-

'What was William wearing?' she asked, holding it up.

The colour drained from David's face. 'I've lost him,' he whispered, slumping against the tree.

Chapter Eighteen

Jacen sat in the kitchen, finishing his cup of tea. It was early, but his dad was already out milking the cows, and his mum had gone into the office ahead of time. He stared at the steam curling from his mug, wondering what to say to Willow. He'd been short with her the other day — no, if he was honest, he'd shouted — and he hated leaving it like that.

She'd gone to Canada, and William had told him yesterday that Lilly was there now too.

Jacen wandered across the farmyard, boots crunching on the gravel. The morning was cool and quiet, apart from the distant lowing of cattle. He drifted towards the old barn and climbed up onto a big round straw bale, pulling out his phone.

10.17, Jacen:
Sorry I shouted at you. Please forgive me.

10.18, Willow:
I forgive you, already forgotten.

. . .

10.19, Jacen:
You missed Jake's party. It was no fun without you. He was
disappointed.

10.20, Willow:
Wasn't allowed to go in case I electrocuted someone

10.21, Jacen:
Oh, ok maybe not then, would have been funny though. When are you coming home? Miss you.

10.22, Willow:
Miss you too. Can't wait until Mum thinks I'm safe xxx

Jacen smiled faintly, tucked his phone away and lay back, folding his hands behind his head. The barn smelled faintly of hay and old timber. For a while, all he could hear was the wind moving through the yard.

Then the dog started barking. It wasn't his usual bark at a passing tractor or a wandering sheep. This was sharp, angry — a warning.

Jacen sat up. His breath caught. Four men stood at the edge of the yard, watching him. They hadn't been there a moment ago.

Their skin was unnaturally dark, as if shadow clung to it, and their stillness made the hairs on the back of his neck rise.

'Um... can I help you? This is private property,' he called, trying to keep his voice steady.

They didn't answer. Slowly, they began to smile. The smiles stretched too wide, showing teeth that were jagged and wrong.

Jacen's stomach lurched. Willow had told him about dark elves —and suddenly he knew, without doubt, that's what they were.

He slid down from the bale, forcing his legs not to shake.

'What do you want?'

'We want you, human,' the nearest one rasped, his voice like dry leaves scraping on stone.

'I'm no one important,' Jacen managed, though his heart was hammering.

'Enough questions,' the elf snarled, eyes glinting red in the morning light. 'Come with us willingly, or we make you. And I promise — you don't want that.'

The others moved in, fast and silent. Jacen turned to run, but a hand like iron clamped onto his arm. Another caught his shoulder.

The dog's barking rose to a furious pitch, but it was already too late.

'Let me go!' Jacen shouted, struggling against their grip. They didn't even seem to notice.

They dragged him towards the shade cast by the barn, the world narrowing to the pressure on his arms, the stink of leather and cold air.

The last thing he heard was the dog's desperate barking — before the shadows swallowed him whole.

Hàlfr didn't bother knocking before he strode into Lord Hurleston's office. Even this late, the old elf was still at his desk, reading by the light of a single lamp.

'Sir, Laran and Lilly are barricaded in the house in Canada, trying to stop the dark elves from taking Willow and Gail. I've already spoken to Andarta — William's been taken despite her and David's best efforts,' Hàlfr said without preamble.

'Oh, my goodness. Disturbing, of course,' Hurleston replied, unruffled. 'But it begs the question — what you're still doing here?'

'Sir?' Hàlfr asked, caught off guard.

'Laran and Mother Nature need your help. Put together a tactical team and get over there. I'll alert our local assets and hope they can hold out until you and the cavalry arrive,' Hurleston said sharply.

'There's something else,' Hàlfr added grimly. 'They've taken the human boy, Jacen, as well.'

Hurleston's brows rose. 'Is that so? Curious... Why on earth would they do that?' He shook his head. 'Oh well — we'll puzzle it out later. Right now, you need to move. I'll speak to Marcion.

He's been tracking all the dark elf cells that became active after the castle attack — perhaps he can tell me exactly what game they're playing. Now, go.'

Laran unlocked one cabinet and took out an SA80 Bullpup assault rifle, identical to the sort used by the British Army. He passed it to Gail, along with a bulletproof vest and some combat webbing to hold extra magazines of ammunition. Lilly looked at them both with exasperation.

'Doesn't mum need a weapon?' Asked Willow as she slipped on her body armour.

'No darling, I don't need a gun. A sword would be useful, though,' she raised an eyebrow at Laran. He grinned and opened another cabinet, passing Lilly a sword. She balanced it in her hand, feeling the weight of it. He then handed her a scabbard and belt for the sword.

'Thanks.' For some reason, the thought of getting into a proper scrap with some dark elves appealed to her.

'So, dad, what's the plan?' Gail asked, unable to keep the excitement out of his voice.

'Well, I suggest we have something to eat and discuss our options. If they are dark elves, they won't be able to get in here until evening, when the shadows are at the longest and the light is at its worst. First, we need to go around and make sure every light in the house is on. Hopefully, when they realise they can't get in that way, and can't force their way in, they'll give up,' Laran said with a grin.

'Do you really think they will, dad?' Gail asked.

'Hopefully, whilst you two are turning the lights on, I'll get on the satellite phone to Hàlfr and let him know what's going on.'

'Sounds like a plan to me,' Lilly said. Willow and Gail walked upstairs to turn the lights on. Willow sat on Gail's bed. Gail sat down next to her. He could see, by her expression, that she was frightened. He put his arm around her and pulled her against him.

'Are you okay?' Gail asked gently.

'Yeah... why are they here? Are they after us again? Will we never be safe?' Willow put her arm around Gail as he gently kissed her. It was tricky in the combat armour.

'I don't know. But Dad will keep us safe, and I have a feeling your mom can handle herself in a fight,' Gail smiled, making Willows mouth tremble with a tentative smile.

'If it gets really bad, there is a panic room hidden under Mom's library,' he said, trying to reassure her.

Laran wandered into the kitchen and smiled as he watched Lilly cook.

'Need a hand?' He asked as he walked over to the stove and peered into the pan.

'Excuse me, are you interfering with my cooking? No, I don't need a hand. But you could set the table.' Lilly smiled as Laran stepped away from the stove.

'Wouldn't dream of messing with Mother Nature and her cooking,' Laran replied sarcastically as he took the cutlery out of a drawer.

'Laran, what's going on? They want Gail, don't they?' Lilly watched Laran.

'I think they do, and I am not sure why.' Laran confessed.

'So, this isn't about the reason you have hidden him?' Lilly looked at Laran.

'No, I think this is to do with the Elder Council. I think the dark elves want to take the children to distract us from something else,' Laran said grimly.

'What though? What are we missing and who is coordinating all of this?' Lilly mused as she dished up the salmon steaks and potatoes. By then, Willow and Gail had walked in.

'So, Dad, what's the plan?' Gail asked, pushing his plate away and sitting back, sipping his beer.

'The plan is we defend you and Willow until Hàlfr gets here,'

'That's it?' Gail asked in disbelief.

'Yeah, pretty much.' Laran replied nonchalantly.

'Wow, Dad, your plans still suck,' Gail chuckled.

'Hey, if you are referring to Uncle Ashes birthday, that was a sound plan,' Laran defended, his eyes sparkling with mirth.

'Yeah, Dad, you tell yourself that, but we lost,' Gail chuckled.

After dinner, they all retreated to the lounge and watched T.V. to stop the tension from getting to them. Some hours later, the dark elves still hadn't attacked, and Gail was bored.

'What the hell are they waiting for? It's been hours,' Gail demanded as he stood up and paced around in frustration.

'Maybe it was a false alarm?' Lilly gestured from the couch.

'Perhaps,' Laran agreed. 'You two, it's late; you should probably go to bed. If nothing has happened by the morning, we'll lower the defences and try to figure out what's going on.' At the top of the stairs, Willow stopped. 'Can I sleep with you, please?'

'Yeah, sure. Might be best and safer. Um, no hanky panky,' Gail smiled. Willow burst out laughing.

'Hanky panky,' she gasped between giggles as Gail placed his hands on his hips and looked hurt. They got into bed, snuggling against each other. 'Gail, I'm scared. Why do they want us?' Willow whispered, feeling his arm tighten around her.

'Your mum and my dad will protect us, and what they want, I don't know. I will look after you.' Gail moved so he could kiss her, pulling her against him. He tucked her head under his chin, putting his arms around her as she fell asleep. Gail was far to wound up to sleep.

The explosion woke Lilly with a start. The sound was deafening and shook the entire house. She jumped out of bed and got dressed as quickly as she could. The house alarm was blaring loudly. She stepped out into the corridor to see Gail rushing up the corridor, assault rifle raised.

'Looks like it wasn't a false alarm after all,' he said cheerily as he rushed past her, Willow in tow.

'That sounded like it came from the east side of the house, probably the dining room,' Lilly said as she followed them down the stairs and into the lounge area. It was deserted, and they could hear gunfire emanating from the corridor leading to the dining room.

'Gail, take Willow to the library and seal yourselves in the panic room. Only come out when I say, no matter what you hear, okay?' Lilly commanded as she drew her sword.

'Yes, Mum,' Willow replied. They hurried off in the opposite direction towards the library.

Lilly continued down the corridor towards the dining room to find Laran leaning against the door frame and firing his weapon into the room. Lilly leaned up against the wall on the other side of the door frame and looked over at him.

'What's the situation?' She asked as he retreated around the doorframe just in time to avoid a hail of gunfire.

'So, they've blown a hole in the outside wall and are trying to fight their way in. So far, I've got things under control, but there's no telling how much explosives they've got. If they blow their way into other rooms, we're going to have a problem,' he said grimly.

'We need to clear the dining room and make them think

twice before coming into the house. Are you feeling up to a bit of close quarters combat?' He asked as he unclipped a flash bang from his belt, put his gun down and drew his sword.

'I guess so,' Lilly replied nervously.

'Well, that's good enough for me. Close your eyes and cover your ears. As soon as it goes off, we're going in,' he instructed, before pulling the pin and throwing the flash bang into the room.

As soon as it went off, she charged into the dining room with Laran. The dark elves were still stunned and put up no resistance until Lilly and Laran were right amongst them. By then it was too late, their assault rifles near useless at such close range and with too little time to draw their own swords. Lilly and Laran mercilessly cut down the ones that weren't intelligent enough to flee back into the grounds.

After what seemed like little more than a heartbeat to Lilly, the fighting was over. The air was thick with ozone and the floor was littered with the bodies of six dark elves. She looked around to see Laran covered in blood and grinning at her, truly reminiscent of some ancient god of war. His grisly visage slightly shocked her when she realised that she probably looked little better.

'What now?' She asked as she sheathed her bloody blade.

'Now, we wait for round two,' he replied as he sheathed his own weapon and walked back out into the corridor to retrieve his assault rifle.

'Gail, this isn't the way to the library,' Willow gasped as she ran after Gail.

'Yes, it is. Just not the most direct route,' Gail said, coming to a sudden stop. He felt along the wall, and there, carefully concealed, was a door. Gail carefully reached for Willow's hand and pulled her through.

'Wow, Gail. This is so cool,' whispered Willow.

'Yeah, Dad put all this in when the house was built. Used to hide in here when I was a kid,' Gail smiled back. 'Come on,' he led her along the narrow passage.

Chapter Nineteen

Gail pushed the door open and peered into the library; gunfire rattled from the other end of the house. The place was a mess, shelves toppled, books scattered everywhere. Through a jagged hole blown in the wall, more dark elves were streaming in, weapons ready.

Gail's gut tightened. There was no way they could make it to the panic room now.

He shut the door and turned to Willow. 'We've got a problem.

Dark elves between us and the panic room. Assault rifle or no, I don't fancy our chances.'

'So, what do we do?' Willow asked, trying not to let her voice shake.

'Back the way we came. Link up with Mum and Dad, tell them they're about to be surrounded.' His expression was grim.

Lilly and Laran had barricaded the dining-room door, buying themselves precious minutes. In the kitchen, Lilly spotted blood

on Laran's arm and grabbed a clean tea towel, tearing it into strips.

'Here, let me—'

He smiled at her, about to make some quip, when he suddenly shoved her to the floor and dropped on top of her. Machine-gun fire ripped through the cupboards, glass shattering, wood splintering.

Laran rolled away, returning fire in short bursts. One dark elf dropped, another went down wounded. The rest retreated into the lounge, firing blindly into the kitchen from cover.

Willow and Gail slipped out of the secret passage. The corridor was empty, but gunfire echoed from the lounge. Gail pressed a finger to his lips, then edged forward.

Six dark elves. Two at the kitchen door, firing. Two crouched over a wounded comrade. One more sprawled, clearly dead.

Gail exhaled, raised his weapon, and pivoted into the doorway. Three precise shots — the two at the kitchen door collapsed, then the one tending the wounded. The last ablebodied dark elf fired wildly, but Gail was already back in cover.

He didn't get far. A beam of pure sunlight slammed into his chest, sending him sprawling. Smoke curled from Lilly's fingers as she strode into the lounge, Laran behind her, finishing the wounded elf with his sword.

'Good shot back there,' Laran said.

'Thanks. Not sure how much longer I can keep this up,' Lilly admitted. Her skin was pale, eyes shadowed.

'Why aren't you two in the panic room?' she demanded when Gail and Willow slipped in.

'We can't get there — they're in the library,' Willow said.

'That'll be where this lot came from,' Laran muttered. He nodded to Gail. 'Good shooting, son.'

'Thanks, but more will be here any second. We need a plan.'

'We can't shoot our way to the panic room,' Laran decided.

'Upstairs. Make them fight up the staircase — one hell of a bottleneck.'

'I agree,' Lilly said. 'Let's move.'

Hàlfr and his men were already circling the woods. The house looked gutted, muzzle flashes flaring in its windows. Flashes of sunlight lit the upstairs like a beacon — Lilly, for sure.

On his signal, they slipped forward, silencing the few dark elf sentries with swift, lethal precision. But there was still a wall of enemies between them and the house.

'Open fire,' Hàlfr ordered. The night erupted in gunfire.

Upstairs, the change in sound was immediate.

'Dad, I think Hàlfr's here,' Gail said, relief breaking across his face. Lilly sat with her back to the wall, eyes closed. She'd burned through most of her energy.

'How much ammo left?' Laran asked.

'None.' Gail lifted his sword. Willow huddled beside him.

'Then we sit tight. Let him fight his way in.'

'Seriously? We've fought all night and you want to wait?' Gail stared.

'Maybe you're right. Could be time for a killing blow.' Laran's grin was all teeth.

'Are you completely mad?' Lilly snapped. 'You're not going out there, and neither is Gail.'

'We'll be back before you know it,' Laran said, already moving. Gail followed, grinning like a maniac. Lilly swore under her breath and pulled Willow along after them.

Hàlfr's team swept through the library, cutting down stragglers. It was almost too easy, and that worried him.

In the wrecked kitchen, Laran eased through into the living room — straight into the muzzle of Hàlfr's rifle.

'Don't shoot!' Laran barked.

Hàlfr's mouth twitched into a smile as he lowered it. 'Good to see you in one piece.'

'No thanks to you,' Laran muttered.

'Annie's going to love the redecorating,' Hàlfr said, glancing at the bullet-riddled walls.

'Yeah, well, maybe if you'd got here sooner...' Laran chuckled.

'Everyone alright?' Hàlfr asked, scanning them.

'Just tired and bruised,' Lilly replied.

'Glad you kept your dad out of trouble, Gail,' Hàlfr teased. 'He's useless in a fight.'

'You're just jealous,' Laran shot back, clapping him on the shoulder.

Willow shrugged off her vest and collapsed onto what was left of the sofa. Lilly sat beside her.

'You alright, darling?' she asked softly.

'Yeah... but why us? What have we done?'

'Nothing,' Lilly said firmly, pulling her close. She glanced at Gail, already dozing in an armchair, and shook her head.

While Laran, Hàlfr, and the team swept the grounds for any lingering dark elves, the lounge was quiet — just the sound of breathing and the occasional creak of boots on ruined floorboards.

Chapter Twenty

Lord Malcor crouched in the shade a few metres from the edge of the tree line. Covered from head to toe in foliage and twigs, he was almost invisible to the untrained eye. He had been there all night, watching as the first wave of his troops laid siege to the Autumn King's home.

He'd seen them blow their way inside and listened patiently to the gunfire and explosions that echoed from within. He had even remained perfectly still when the Autumn King's reinforcements — led by his second-in-command — ghosted silently through the forest, passing within metres of his hiding place.

Malcor had smiled as they attacked his men and entered the house. They had fallen for his trap perfectly. Hàlfr's force numbered little more than twenty. Well-armed and experienced though they were, they would be no match for his full strength.

He rose to a crouch and keyed his radio.

'The trap is set. Advance with the second wave. Capture the Autumn Prince and the Child of Nature. Use as much force as necessary.'

Through his binoculars he watched fifty dark elves, accompanied by two brutish dark elf ogres, emerge from the far side of the forest and begin their assault.

Lilly jumped to her feet as the elves and ogres stormed into the room. She grabbed Willow and managed to dash out just in time to avoid being cut down by a withering hail of machine-gun fire.

Gail wasn't as lucky. The living room wall collapsed inwards, throwing him hard to the floor. Dazed, he lay still, listening to the chaos of gunfire around him. Something warm trickled down his temple — a piece of the wall had cut his head. Worse, the debris had pinned his legs. Only the over-turned chair beside him had spared his upper body from worse injury.

Lilly raced down the corridor towards the direction Laran and Hàlfr had gone. Sporadic bursts of gunfire echoed from ahead — close. She skidded to a halt as a group of Hàlfr's men came running out of a room and stopped in front of her.

'Ma'am, you can't go that way. King Autumn has instructed us to get you and the children out to safety.'

'We can't go back. We need another way out,' Lilly snapped.

'Mum, what about Gail? We can't just leave him!' Willow's voice cracked with fear.

'We can't help him right now. Getting you to safety is the priority,' Lilly said firmly. She turned to the nearest soldier. 'Send one of your men back to King Autumn and tell him his son is unaccounted for. The rest of you — defend the Child of Nature. I have a plan.'

Laran and Hàlfr were pinned down in the wreck of the library, crouched behind a fallen bookcase. The thump of heavy footfalls shook the floor as a dark elf ogre smashed its way towards them, destroying everything in its path.

'There's a passage in the wall. We need to get to it,' Laran muttered, ducking down to reload.

'Lead the way. I was bored of reading anyway,' Hàlfr grinned, following as Laran crawled along the floor, using the toppled shelves as cover.

He felt along the far wall until his fingers found a concealed handle, pushed it open, and slipped inside. Hàlfr and his surviving men followed quickly, emerging into the adjoining study — and finding Lilly trapped inside.

They caught the dark elves in the room completely by surprise. Moving fast, Laran used one of his lesser-known gifts as

King of the Autumn Elves — a touch to the back of the neck that dropped all six to the floor without a sound. He stepped over them.

'I hear you've lost my son,' he said quietly, looking pointedly at Lilly.

'I wouldn't say lost exactly. I know where he probably is. I just can't get to him.' Lilly's glare softened when Laran grinned.

'Best go and get him then, hadn't we?'

'Laran, we can't beat these lot head-on — not alone. But I've got an idea, and I'll need your help.'

'Go on,' he said, breathing hard.

'I need you to help me clear the library and lay down covering fire so I can make a dash to the tree line.'

'May I ask why?'

'Oh, you'll see. Now come on, we haven't got all day.'

Together, Laran, Lilly, Hàlfr and five Autumn Elves charged into the library, catching its dark elf occupants off guard.

Laran, Hàlfr, and the elves opened fire immediately. At the same time, Lilly summoned every scrap of energy she had left and unleashed a concentrated beam of sunlight into the ogre's face.

The monster bellowed in agony, staggered backwards, and toppled.

Seizing the moment, Laran sprinted from cover, sword drawn, leapt onto the ogre's chest and drove the blade down into its skull.

With their brute felled, the dark elves' morale shattered. They broke and fled back through the blasted gap in the wall.

Hàlfr and his elves chased them into the garden, cutting down the stragglers and clearing that side of the grounds.

'Lilly — you won't get a better chance than this,' Hàlfr called over his shoulder.

She nodded, jogged to the gap in the wall, and slipped through. Seconds later, she was sprinting across the open lawn towards the tree line, vanishing into the shadows of the woods.

Chapter Twenty-One

King Spring took the steps to his house two at a time, his mind still crackling with the urgency of Lord Hurleston's call. The news had been grim — and it was about to get worse.

He was halfway up when the front door burst open. Hyacinth flew down towards him, skirts whipping around her legs, and launched herself into his arms.

'Papa!' she gasped, relief and delight in her voice.

Sixteen years old, and already the picture of poise — but her long, wavy black hair framed eyes that held the same violet-blue fire as her mother's, and a perfect pale complexion that would stop hearts in every season from here to Winter. She was, without question, the jewel of his family.

'Hyacinth, my dear,' he said, holding her tightly for a moment longer than usual.

She drew back and searched his face. 'What brings you here?'

It struck her, not for the first time, that they looked more like siblings than grandfather and granddaughter. King Spring's wavy black hair was untouched by grey, and his striking blue eyes were exactly mirrored in hers.

'I need to speak to your father,' he said, though his voice lacked its usual playfulness. 'And where's your brother?'

'Dad's in his study. Leaf's...' she rolled her eyes, trying to mask her irritation, '...probably out charming some poor girl.

He's so like you. Mother despairs; Daddy just laughs.'

She took his hand, and together they went inside.

Harry was waiting in the study, rising from behind his desk as they entered. Broad-shouldered and handsome, his hair — the same black waves as his father and daughter — was now flecked with grey. His face was open, friendly, but the set of his jaw told King Spring he'd been bracing for bad news.

'You got my message?' King Spring asked without preamble.

Harry nodded. 'Yes. This must be serious to drag you all the way here and off that yacht of yours.' 'It's not a boat, it's a yacht,' King Spring said automatically, before his smile faded. 'You know about the kidnapping in the summer — Hyperion's work.'

'Of course. It was in all the papers. I imagine Laran was thrilled to have Gail plastered across the front page. But that's history. Why are you here now?'

'Because that was only the warm-up.' King Spring's eyes hardened.

'The dark elves are moving again. They have William. At this very moment, Laran and Mother Nature are fighting to stop them from taking Gail and Willow. A human boy has been taken too. And Hurleston thinks your children may be next.'

Harry's face drained of colour. 'What? Why—'

A sharp knock at the door interrupted him. One of his Spring Elf commanders entered, saluted, and spoke in a clipped voice.

'Sir, a pack of dark elves just tried to enter the village. When my men barred the way, they demanded your children — immediately. They say if we don't hand them over, they'll take them by force.'

'Hold them off,' Harry said, the steel in his voice leaving no room for doubt. 'Kill any who try to cross the boundary.'

'We'll delay them as long as we can,' the commander said grimly.

King Spring stepped forward. 'Harry, you can't hold them off forever. You don't have the numbers. If you fight, this village will drown in blood. Give them the children.'

Harry turned on him, eyes blazing. 'You're asking me to hand over my own children!'

'I'm asking you to save your people,' King Spring shot back.

'We'll get them back. They won't harm them — not yet. But if you force the elves' hand, you'll be burying half the village by nightfall.'

Harry's hands clenched. His gaze shifted to the commander, then back to his father. Slowly, painfully, he gave the order. 'Tell them a small party may enter to take the children. Keep them under guard. Make sure no harm comes to anyone else.'

The commander saluted and left.

Harry stood in silence for a moment, then called out, 'Cyn, come here, darling.'

She appeared almost instantly, her expression stricken — she'd heard everything.

'Fetch your brother,' Harry said gently. 'Stay calm, do as they say. We'll find you. You just have to be brave.'

Her chin trembled but she nodded. 'Leaf won't like this,' she whispered, before hurrying off.

Leaf arrived moments later, taller by a head than his sister, but carrying the same black hair and piercing blue eyes. 'What's going on? Cyn says we're—' His gaze snapped to his father.

'You're giving us to them?'

'I have no choice. There are too many. Look after your sister. I swear we will bring you home.'

Harry took their hands and led them to the front door.

Outside, the dark elves were already approaching — tall, lean figures with cruel, glittering eyes and armour that drank in the light. Cyn pressed into her brother's side. Leaf's arms wrapped protectively around her, his glare locked on the enemy as they closed in.

The dark elves fanned out as they neared the house, their formation loose but purposeful. The air seemed to grow colder with every step they took. Cyn tightened her grip on Leaf's sleeve.

Up close, the elves were even worse than she remembered from the whispered stories — armour like liquid shadow clung to their bodies, and their faces were pale and sharp, mouths curled into cold half-smiles. Their eyes were black wells with flecks of red, inhuman and unreadable.

One of them stepped forward. He was taller than the rest, his black hair tied back, his throat etched with curling designs that looked disturbingly like vines with thorns.

'The Spring Prince and Princess,' he said, his voice a rasp that slithered over the skin. 'You have them ready?'

Harry stepped in front of his children. 'They are to be returned unharmed. You have my word as their father — and you will have the wrath of my court if—'

'Save your speeches, elf,' the dark elf cut him off, his gaze flicking to King Spring with something between recognition and disdain. 'Your father knows the rules of the game. We take them now.'

Leaf stiffened. 'I'm not.'

'Leaf,' King Spring said sharply, his voice low but carrying the weight of a command. Leaf bit off whatever he was going to say, but his jaw locked tight.

The leader extended a long-fingered hand, and two of his warriors stepped forward. The movement was silent, practised. Cyn's heart was hammering so loud she was sure everyone could hear it. She forced herself to look at her father, to hold his gaze. He nodded once. It was all she needed — and all she could bear.

'Stay together,' Harry murmured to them both, and then he let go.

The dark elves closed in, their hands cold and firm on Cyn's and Leaf's arms.

'We will find you!' Harry called after them, his voice breaking despite himself.

Leaf twisted his head enough to glare back at the elves. 'You'd better hope they do,' he muttered.

The leader gave a thin smile. 'Oh, they will find you. The question is — when.'

Without another word, they turned and began the march out of the village. Villagers had gathered along the edges of the path,
silent and stricken, some clutching each other, others bowing their heads.

King Spring and Harry stood shoulder to shoulder, watching until the dark figures slipped into the tree line and were swallowed by the shadows.

Only then did Harry speak. 'If they hurt them.'

'They won't,' King Spring said, but his tone was grim. 'Not yet. They still want something.'

'And you know what that something is?'

King Spring's eyes stayed on the forest. 'No. But we're about to find out.'

Chapter Twenty-Two

G ail lay still beneath the rubble, dust choking his lungs.

Through a narrow gap he could just see the ogre crashing around in the wreckage. The elves it had come with had scattered into the rest of the house.

He wriggled his legs. Nothing. They were pinned. He tried again, harder, and felt a faint movement in his foot—relief, but not much. His gun was nowhere in sight.

'Uuugh,' the ogre grunted. Gail froze, willing himself silent. A sudden crash tore through the air. The ogre shoved aside a chunk of wall, revealing Gail's face. For lack of a better plan, he offered it a shaky smile.

'Nice ogre... I'm Gail. What's your name?' The creature stared, baffled for a heartbeat—then roared, hot, foul breath spraying across Gail's face.

'Oh, damn,' he muttered, bracing for the end.

Laran arrived like a storm—charging full pelt, firing from the hip at the few elves still in the lounge. Miraculously, none of their shots hit him as he made straight for the ogre. He slammed into it like a rugby tackle—only to bounce straight off and sprawl on the floor.

The ogre roared again and lumbered towards him. Hàlfr and his men poured into the room, guns blazing—but fresh dark elves swarmed through the gap in the wall, forcing them into a firefight.

Laran drew his sword and met the ogre head-on, bellowing as he ducked under a sweeping arm. His blade slashed deep gashes into its gut and chest, but the thing only grew angrier.

A massive swing missed his head by inches, but when he dodged the next, he slammed straight into its enormous foot. The impact knocked him sideways, and before he could recover, the ogre's hand closed around his throat and lifted him to eye level.

Thinking fast, Laran stabbed it in the eye. It howled, flinging him across the room into what was left of a wall. His ribs screamed in protest as he tried to stand.

That was all Hàlfr's men needed—gunfire tore into the ogre-muntil it toppled dead.

'Took you long enough,' Hàlfr said with a grin, hauling Laran to his feet.

'Mythical creatures. Damn nuisance,' Laran grunted.

'Where's Gail?'

Laran scanned the room, spotting him under the rubble. 'You planning on lying there all day?' he called.

'Yeah, figured I'd wait for the next ogre to eat me,' Gail shot back weakly. 'Legs are stuck. Can't move.'

Hàlfr and his men hauled him out just as Willow rushed in, wide-eyed.

'We can't get out that way—too many of them. We might have to surrender,' she panted, looking at Laran's bloodied limp.

'Played with an ogre,' he replied with a smirk.

'No way!' Gail shouted, but another wave of elves poured through the wall. He shoved Willow to the floor and they scrambled for the door.

Gunfire tore past. Willow almost made it—until something struck her head. She crumpled.

'Where's Willow?' Gail turned, horror flooding his face at the sight of her lying motionless. He sprinted back, but Hàlfr grabbed his collar and yanked him away.

'You're too important to die for her. Panic room—now!'

'I need to help her!'

'Move!' Hàlfr shoved him towards the library. From his position behind the wreck of a sofa, Laran saw it all —and frowned at Hàlfr's urgency. But there was no time to dwell.

A flashbang went off, deafening the room. In the chaos, Hàlfr's men dragged Willow clear.

'Where's Gail?' Laran demanded.

'With Hansen. Panic room.'

'Not until we look at her head.' Laran crouched beside Willow. Blood streaked her temple, but her eyes fluttered open.

'First aid kit—kitchen,' Hàlfr said, and together they carried her there. His radio crackled with Hansen's voice over distant gunfire:

'Panic room secure. Prince Autumn is safe.'

'Keep him that way,' Hàlfr ordered.

'What's going on?' Laran demanded.

'They're here for him. They must've found out.'

'Found out what?'

'He's not your son. His mother was Lord Bracken's daughter.' Laran froze.

'The dark elf general?'

'After the massacre—they killed James and Jasmine—we took Gail. Bracken was there. Wanted him then. Must've finally given him up.'

'And nobody told me?'

'You weren't there. We kept it quiet.' Laran's chest heaved. 'Fine. Take Willow, get her out. I'll find

Gail.'

'Are you sure you're the right—'

'That's an order. He's still my son.' Sword in hand, he sprinted from the kitchen.

Chapter Twenty-Three

L illy had sprinted into the forest, calling as she went. She stopped to catch her breath just as a huge grizzly ambled toward her.

'Mother Nature, how may I be of assistance?' the bear rumbled.

'Child of Nature is under attack and requires your assistance.

Can you mobilise more bears to help you?'

'Of course, Mother Nature.' With a respectful bow of its head, the bear let out a deep, rolling bellow. All around, more bears emerged from the shadows of the trees.

'Where do you wish us to go?'

'Do you know the house of the Autumn King?'

'Of course. Climb up.'

Lilly swung onto the bear's back and gripped its thick fur as it surged forward. Behind them came the pounding footfalls of many animals — deer, wolves, foxes — answering the call and joining the charge.

Inside, Laran moved quickly toward the library. The dark elf onslaught had thinned, but that only set him more on edge. Outside, flashes of bright light flared through the windows, mixed with deep, feral growls. He ignored it for now and pushed into the library.

The room was eerily deserted, the once-hidden panic room door now in plain sight. Laran didn't hesitate — he keyed in the code, the lock clicked, and the heavy door swung open. Hansen stood inside with Gail.

'Dad, it's good to see you—' Gail began, but the words froze on his lips.

'Sir, look out!' Hansen shouted, lunging — too late. A crimson-black blade punched clean through Laran's chest. He was yanked backwards, thrown to the floor like a rag doll.

Hansen fired instinctively, the shots cracking loud in the enclosed space, but a second dark elf burst through and drove a blade into him. The corporal's expression flickered from shock to nothing as he collapsed.

Gail grabbed for his weapon, but the dark elves swarmed him. He fought, kicking and twisting, but they slammed him into the wall, ripped the rifle from his hands, and forced his arms behind his back.

From the shadows stepped Lord Malcor, smiling as though greeting an old friend. He strolled forward and planted a boot beside Laran's head.

'Thank you for opening the door. I would never have got in without you,' he chuckled.

Laran tried to speak, but blood filled his throat. Only a choking gurgle escaped.

'Don't be like that,' Malcor went on, gripping Laran's hair and forcing his gaze upward. 'It's a joyous occasion. For the second time, I get to take what's most precious to the King of the Autumn Elves.'

Laran's vision blurred, the edges going dark. A thunder of boots and claws shook the house. Hàlfr burst into the library with two of his men — and in his arms, limp and pale, was Willow. Her hair was matted with blood where a bullet had grazed her temple.

A massive grizzly barreled through the gap, roaring, its flanks bristling with wolves. Lilly leapt from its back, sunlight sparking at her fingertips, her eyes locking on the sight of Willow in Hàlfr's arms... and Gail, bound and bleeding, being dragged toward the hole in the wall.

'Lilly!' Hàlfr's voice cracked. 'She's alive, but—'

'No!' she shouted.

The animals tore into the nearest dark elves, the air thick with snarls and the clash of claws on armour. But Malcor didn't flinch — his eyes stayed on Gail.

'We finally have another chance to destroy the abomination. The emperor will be most pleased.' The dark elves shoved Gail ahead of them. Willow stirred faintly before going limp again.

Laran tried to push himself upright, blood pooling beneath him. 'Gail!' he roared, voice raw.

Gail twisted his head, meeting his father's eyes for one fleeting moment — and then he was gone, swallowed into the chaos outside.

Lilly spun, sunlight blazing in her hands, but the gap in the wall was already empty. The forest swallowed them, leaving only the sound of retreating footsteps... and the echo of Laran's broken cry.

They forced him out into the night, through the ragged gap in the wall and into the forest beyond. Rain dripped from the leaves above, the cold air burning in his lungs as they half-dragged, half- shoved him between the trees. The smell of damp earth and smoke clung to everything.

Gail stumbled once, twice, his legs barely cooperating, but the elves yanked him upright each time. Malcor kept glancing back, his smile sharp in the dim light. After several minutes, they reached a small clearing where more dark elves waited.

'No more struggling, boy,' Malcor said, stepping close. Then, without ceremony, he slammed the pommel of his sword into the side of Gail's head. White-hot pain flared — and the world went black.

T H E E N D

Continued in part four.
A sneak preview
Springs Revelation

C M Stolworthy

SPRING'S
REVELATION

CHAPTER ONE
WINTER CASTLE

Jasmine Aristata smiled as the car travelled along the gravel drive, the crunch beneath the tyres almost a comfort. As the vehicle swung around the curve, the castle came into view—the turrets of the medieval fortress emerging from the mist, giving the scene a magical, mysterious feeling.

'We're almost there, little man,' she said, stroking the baby's soft cheek, a smile transforming her features from anxious to relieved.

Flags bearing the Winter coat of arms fluttered in the breeze atop the turrets. The battlements, once manned with guards, now stood empty—more for show than defence. Butterflies stirred in her stomach as excitement welled up. It felt as though she hadn't seen her friend, Queen Solstice, in years. In reality, it had only been a few months.

The car glided around the ornate fountain and came to a stop at the foot of the imposing stone steps. The chauffeur opened her door and offered his hand. Taking it, Jasmine stepped from the car.

'Thank you.'

'My pleasure.' His paternal smile soothed her nerves about being here.

She glanced up the sweeping stone steps leading to the grand wooden doors, her hand gripping the handle of the baby seat. She braced herself as Queen Winter threw the doors open and descended rapidly.

'Jasmine! How lovely to see you!' Solstice seemed to fly down the steps, her feet barely touching the ground. Her skin was cool as she embraced her friend. 'Let me take the baby.' Solstice gazed down at the sleeping child. 'He's adorable. Are you staying? Say you are—I've missed you so much.'

'Yes, of course I'm staying. Didn't drive all this way just for a coffee.' Jasmine laughed at her friend's enthusiasm.

Following Solstice into the castle, she was grateful to escape the chill. The chauffeur trailed behind, carrying Jasmine's bags and baby paraphernalia, which he set down on the flag stoned floor.

Jasmine's gaze swept over the familiar, opulent surroundings. To her left stood the ornate Tudor staircase, while to her right stretched a plush hallway leading deeper into the castle.

'So, tell me everything. How has motherhood been? And married to that delicious man?' Solstice enquired, leading Jasmine into one of the sitting rooms that overlooked the formal gardens. With the fire blazing in the grate, Jasmine settled into an overstuffed chair as a maid brought in a pot of tea and a tray of sandwiches.

'I mentioned to Taranis that a baby would be nice. He looked positively terrified.' Solstice giggled.

'Oh, you know—he's tiring, although quite well-behaved for a baby. James works as usual. FERA doesn't give him a moment's rest. It's just... I get lonely on my own all day,' Jasmine confessed, watching her friend cuddle the baby. 'Now that he's eight weeks old and more settled, I finally felt I could visit you,' she added brightly, lifting her cup for a sip of tea.

'Yes, so—have you seen Laran since he married? I never thought he would!'

'A few times. Helen's lovely—and desperate to start a family.'

'Goodness, Laran as a dad—that'll be interesting. Nice for you and James, though.'

'Yes, James is happy. He went out with Laran and his human friend the other night.'

'Laran has a human friend?'

'Yes—David. He's a friend of Helen's. James is just so happy right now. It's lovely.'

'Oh, I feel a "but" coming,' Solstice said, raising a brow. She could read Jasmine like a book—they'd been close since before her marriage.

'I was hoping to take a quick look in the library. There's something I need to research.' She placed her cup on its saucer.

'Intriguing—do tell.' Solstice leaned forward with a smile. Her flawless beauty struck Jasmine once more, her expression eager as she cuddled the baby.

'Here—read this,' Jasmine said, snapping out of her reverie and pulling a book from her handbag. She handed it to Solstice, who shifted the baby into a more comfortable position and turned the book over in her hands, frowning at its unfamiliar binding. She ran her fingers over the soft leather, tracing the indentations where the gold leaf had worn away.

'What is it?'

'I'm not entirely sure. I was researching the name "Gaillardia" because it holds significant meaning in our world. There hasn't been a Gaillardia in over a century.' Jasmine closed her eyes briefly. 'Anyway, I found this little book with his name in it. I was hoping it might explain its provenance.'

'And you think there's a connection—between him and this book?'

'I do.' Jasmine smiled at Solstice's intuition.

'Inside, I found this.' She leaned over and opened the book to a marked page. 'When I showed James, he visibly paled. Later, I overheard him on the phone with Andarta—he sounded agitated. I listened in.' Jasmine blushed at the confession. 'He was making her promise to watch over Gail—and to keep him away from someone. A girl, I think. James was afraid—of Laran, of all people. But why would Laran want to harm my son? It doesn't make any sense. When I asked James, he just got more upset. So I let it go... sort of.' She bit her lip, her gaze resting on her friend.

'Only—I did some more digging. And now I understand why he was so agitated. It's my fault. I forgot something very important about my family.' She took a shuddering breath. Solstice waited patiently.

'That book reminded me what we are.'

'What do you mean, *what* you are?' Solstice frowned.

'Which branch of elves I come from.'

'Don't start that racist nonsense—'

'No—it's not that. Not exactly. Oh, I don't know. That's why I need the library.'

'Fascinating. Let's take a look then.' Solstice smiled, trying to reassure her.

Gazing at the text, she read aloud:

The Lily that protects all,
While the Willow may weep,
As the blanket of the sun wraps around,
United with the dark it seeks.
For a sacrifice to love, with a pure heart,
Saving all that is precious in the past, the now,
and the future,

Releases the power to heal that resides inside the seasons.

Then the new king will rise as the willow weeps.

The gift of life the Lily gives as the dark joins the light.

'Wow. That's... something else,' murmured Solstice. 'What do you think it means? Do you think it's current—or just some old poem?'

'I think there's a link—between Mother Nature and my son. When he was born, Rose came and "blessed" him. But I don't think it was a blessing,' Jasmine said.

'What makes you say that?'

'I overheard her speaking to James. He was annoyed—said the Natures always meddled, that they couldn't have his son.' Jasmine took another sip of tea. 'Why would they *want* my son?'

'I don't know, Jasmine—but we'll find out. If that will help.' Solstice's voice was calm, comforting.

'Promise me you'll watch over him—if anything happens. Promise me you'll keep him safe. I know that as heir to the House of Aristata, he'll have to meet Mother Nature one day— but please, just protect him.' Jasmine dabbed at her cheeks with a handkerchief, her unshed tears finally escaping.

'Jasmine, of course I will. But nothing's going to happen. He'll be safe—I promise.' Solstice reached over and squeezed her friend's hand. 'Besides, Rose's granddaughter recently married. From all accounts, she's lovely—kind and gentle. She won't harm him.'

'I know. James said she was dating Laran's human friend— the one he met up with. I keep telling myself I'm just being paranoid. But even my dad and Robert were acting strange the other weekend. It's like... like they all know something. A secret I'm not part of.'

'I'm sure they're just thrilled to finally have a male heir—

after all these years,' Solstice said gently. 'Now, shall we have some tea before this little rascal decides it's feeding time?' She looked down at the sleeping baby and smiled.

'Helen, where are you?' Simon called, striding into the bedroom.

'Oh, honey, you look awful.'

'Thanks, babe. I *feel* awful.'

'Why don't you have a nap while I take this little fella out?' he said, bending down to scoop up their son and settle him on the bed.

'That would be really nice,' Helen sighed, lying back with a grateful groan.

'Right then—come on, let's get our coats on,' Simon said to his two-year-old son, who looked up at him with wide, curious eyes.

The walk to the park was pleasant. The weak spring sunshine had finally made an appearance, and cheerful yellow daffodils bobbed and dipped in the breeze. Simon smiled, watching his son's round eyes take in the world around him.

The park bustled with life—families enjoying the Saturday afternoon sunshine, dogs tugging at leads, and a group of boys engaged in a noisy game of football. The ball skidded across the grass and rolled to a stop in front of Simon. With a deft kick, he sent it back. His son giggled in delight.

'Thanks, mister!' one of the boys shouted, weaving around dog walkers to retrieve the ball.

Simon strolled on, veering into a quieter part of the park.

Spotting a large horse chestnut tree, he slowed, casting a quick glance around. With no one in sight, he approached it.

'Shall we go see Uncle James?' he asked, shifting his son to the opposite hip. He held out his hand and pressed his palm against the bark. With a shimmer of golden light, a door appeared in the trunk—silent, radiant, and waiting. Simon glanced around one last time before stepping into the light.

Knocking on the door, Simon stood back and waited. He heard footsteps before the door finally swung open. James Aristata stood blinking at his friend. Clutching his father's leg, James' young son peered up at the visitors on the doorstep.

'Laran, what brings you here?' James, Lord Aristata, asked as he pulled the door wide to let them inside.

'I need a favour,' Laran replied, stepping past him into the hallway.

'Really? How intriguing,' James said, raising a brow as he closed the door to the study. Laran pulled out a chair and sat down, placing his son on his lap. The other little boy settled on the carpet where a collection of toy cars, soldiers, and horses lay scattered. Laran smiled as the child climbed to his feet and handed him a red toy car.

'For baby,' the boy said with a nod, then returned to his toys.

'Thank you, Gail,' Laran said warmly.

'Wow, hasn't William grown?' James smiled at the toddler.

'Yes, he has. And... it's about William that I've come,' Laran said quickly, a look of fear twisting his features.

'What do you mean? What's wrong with him?' James asked, his gaze flicking to the boy—Laran's image in miniature.

'He was always such a calm baby, and at first we just thought we were lucky. But when Helen took him for his check-ups... well, it became obvious it was more than that.' Laran rubbed a hand over his face. 'He's completely deaf.'

James blinked, stunned by the revelation. *How could the King of the Autumn Elves have anything but a perfect child?*

'Okay... how can I help?'

'I want to link the boys.'

'No. Absolutely not.'

Jasmine's voice cut through the air as she entered with a tray of tea things, setting it on the desk before scooping up her son protectively. Holding Gail close, she glared at the two men.

'Jasmine, please—hear me out,' Laran pleaded.

'I'm sorry this has happened, but I won't let you endanger my son.'

'Jasmine, don't be so dramatic—' James began, instantly realising he'd said the wrong thing.

'Don't *patronise* me, James Aristata. And don't think of pulling rank, *King* Laran,' she added with an icy glare.

'Jasmine, it won't hurt them—and it would help William so much. They were going to be friends anyway. This would just... cement the alliance,' Laran reasoned. 'Gail would be a Guardian. William would be able to hear.'

'And Helen? How does she feel about this?' Jasmine demanded.

'She can't know. She knows nothing of the elves, and she can't—if she did, they'd come for her. And with William's... imperfection... the elves would shun him. You know that.'

Laran's voice wavered with fear.

'I'm sorry I shouted. Here let me have a cuddle,' Jasmine

said gently, lifting William from Laran's lap and smiling at the boy. 'Hello, sweetheart. Would you like a cookie?'

William looked to his father, his chin wobbling.

'He can't hear you,' Laran said, signing to his son. William nodded.

'Yes—he would like a cookie.'

'Mummy, cookie please,' Gail added, his voice hopeful.

'Okay, come on you two. Let's get cookies.'

'Thank you, Jasmine,' Laran said softly.

'Don't thank me yet,' she replied, disappearing with the boys.

'Still got fire, that one,' Laran chuckled.

'Yeah... makes me proud. You know the Dark Kings came from her line,' James said, as casually as he could.

'Really? We haven't had one of those in centuries. Can't even remember the last. Why mention it now?'

'Oh, um—Jasmine's sister is getting married.'

'Yes, I saw the announcement. Dylan's a good elf. I've worked with him. Hàlfr speaks highly of him.'

'Who else did you consider as Guardian for William?'

'Taranis suggested one of his Winter Lords. Has a boy the right age.'

'But you'd prefer an Autumn Lord.'

'Yes. You know the traditions. And it would put the House of Aristata in an excellent position,' Laran argued, trying to keep the desperation from his voice. 'Please, Jasmine...'

He trailed off as she returned with the children.

'He missed his daddy,' Jasmine said, handing William back to Laran.

'Who would do it?' James asked.

'After *everything* I've said, you'd still consider it?' Jasmine turned on her husband, her expression a mix of anger and disbelief.

'Jasmine, it's not that unusual. He's the Autumn King's son —and my best friend. Why wouldn't we? The elves would *expect* it. They'd question it if we *didn't*,' James reasoned. 'They'll sit on the Council together, eventually.'

He stood and wrapped his wife and son in his arms.

'Will Rose do it?' she asked quietly.

'Yes. She's already suggested it.'

'And the Elder Council? Do they agree?'

'I haven't approached them yet. Taranis only brought it up after your visit.'

'What does Annie think?'

'That's the strange part. She was hesitant for ages—you know what she's like. Something's been bothering her for a while. Spends all her time in the FERA archive. She tried to talk me out of it at first. But then she came to my office and said we *should* do it. Said it would be good for William, for Gaillardia, and for the House of Autumn. She wouldn't say what changed her mind—but she promised to watch over the boys.'

Jasmine hesitated.

'Okay,' she said finally. 'If Annie believes it's safe, then... I won't stop you.'

'Thank you, Jasmine. This means the world to me.'

'When will it be done?'

'Helen wants to have William christened—it's a human tradition. Rose suggested we do it then.'

Laran stood, the relief evident in his features.

'Thank you, Jasmine. I promise—I'll train this young man personally,' he added, ruffling Gail's hair. The boy giggled.

James saw Laran out and returned to the kitchen, where Jasmine was waiting. She rounded on him immediately.

'He doesn't know, does he?'

'Of course not. Jasmine, this will *help* Gail. If he's

connected to King Laran's son, no one will question his heritage.'

'What if he meets *her*?' Jasmine bit her lip, all her fears surfacing.

'He will, eventually. But it'll be fine. Linked to the Autumn heir, he'll be protected. He'll inherit my title, and your sister's child will inherit your father's. He's safe.'

James pulled his wife close.

'I hope so,' she whispered. 'Because this is dangerously close to treason. And I know Laran wouldn't hesitate to kill Gail if he found out.'

'Then we make sure he *never* finds out. And Gail will be guardian-linked—protected.'

'Oh, James... I hope you're right.'

CHAPTER TWO
PRESENT DAY

Lord Bracken strode through the open doors of the throne room. Architecturally speaking, it was a strange creation. A deep red carpet had been rolled over the original stone floor, stretching from the doorway to the raised platform where Emperor Maleficas' throne now stood.

The palace itself had once been a Buddhist temple. A large golden statue had once stood where the Emperor's throne now commanded the room. Bracken reflected on this as he walked the length of the carpet, the contrast between past serenity and present power striking him once again.

He stopped at the base of the three steps leading to the Emperor's dais.

'My Lord Emperor,' he said, bowing his head with formal reverence.

'Rise, Lord Bracken. We have much to discuss. No doubt you've heard of Lord Malcor's victory?' the Emperor asked, fixing Bracken with his dark crimson gaze. His eyes, Bracken noted, rarely looked human these days.

'Yes, my Emperor—although, had someone informed me sooner, I may have been able to assist Lord Malcor in his efforts,'

Bracken replied, raising his head to meet the Emperor's gaze. 'As I understand it, they forced him to retreat.'

The Emperor lounged on a throne that, Bracken was fairly certain, had been forged from the melted remnants of the old Buddha statue. Two Dark Elf guards stood flanking the throne in full ceremonial plate, their long, jagged black spears—seemingly carved from single shards of flint—held vertically. *Ostentatious*, Bracken thought.

'True, he did,' Maleficas conceded, 'but not before capturing King Autumn's elf, Mother Nature's son, and shooting—killing—the Mother Nature-to-be.'

'My sources indicate that, though injured, the Child of Nature survived,' Bracken countered.

'Is that so... no matter. Lord Malcor's troops also incapacitated King Autumn and destroyed his home. To call anything less than a victory would be an insult to the effort expended.'

'Yes, my Lord Emperor. However, the attack on King Autumn's residence in Canada was one of the largest Dark Elf deployments since the war's end. The humans have been placed on high alert. They'll devote every resource to tracking down the kidnapped children—and Lord Malcor,' Bracken warned.

Maleficas smirked.

'You're correct, Lord Bracken. That is precisely why I intend to use the captives as political prisoners. Their desperate search for the children and Autumn's remnants will blind them to my *other* activities. You and Lord Alloces will meet with Lord Malcor and take custody of some of his prisoners. Divided, they'll be far harder to track.'

'Yes, my Lord Emperor. May I ask... what other activities are you attempting to distract them from?' Bracken asked, voice cautious.

The Emperor narrowed his eyes, his gaze sharpening like a

blade. For a moment, Bracken felt as though his mind were being dissected.

'I've often wondered how far I can trust you, Lord Bracken. At the war's end, yours was the last Dark Elf contingent to recognise my claim to the throne.'

'With respect, my Emperor, my forces and I were deployed to the far side of the world. We were the last to hear what transpired at the siege of the previous Emperor's fortress.'

'Perhaps...' Maleficas said coolly. 'And with Lord Malcor under such intense human scrutiny, I will need your help. Your days on the battlefield may be behind you, but you remain a capable strategist and administrator. I want your assistance moving weapons and troops into Great Britain.'

Bracken's eyes narrowed ever so slightly. 'You would break the Treaty? What of the Elder Council? They will not stand idle. Taking the spring heirs was reckless—the Spring Prince will retaliate.'

'They are weak fools. The taking of the children is distraction enough. And the Spring Prince... his liberal sentiments required a reminder of who he is dealing with.'

'Yes, my lord,' Bracken murmured, bowing once more before turning to leave.

Fool, he thought bitterly as he walked away. *Taking the children was idiotic.*

He would watch how this developed very carefully.

CHAPTER THREE

Gail came to with a jolt, everything crashing back into focus. He staggered to his feet, the crushing reality flooding through him like ice water. William's face swam into view, blurred and doubled. Gail closed his eyes briefly, then reopened them, forcing the two Williams to become one—*the* William he knew.

William reached out to steady him as Gail tentatively touched the bump on his head, wincing as pain flared through his skull. He looked at William and gave a weak smile, swallowing hard. He had no idea what to say.

Willow was dead.

She'd been right. They should have surrendered. He'd last seen his father lying in a pool of blood, a sabre buried in his chest. No one was coming to rescue him. But what did it matter? Nothing mattered.

Willow was gone.

He would never see her again, never hear her laugh at his stupid jokes, never hear her call him an idiot with that sparkle in her eye. His throat tightened. He rubbed his face tiredly and slumped back against the wall.

CHAPTER THREE

'Gail, how're you doing? You've been out for ages,' Leaf asked, his arm wrapped protectively around his sister.

Gail's gaze lifted to the group watching him.

Who were they?

Hyacinth and Leaf—he recognised them by their coal-black hair and violet eyes, clear signs of the royal house of Spring. Another boy sat nearby, scruffy blond hair and soft caramel eyes. Human, not elf, Gail guessed. He didn't know him, but the kind expression required no explanation.

And then his eyes settled on William—Willow's brother, his friend. Dishevelled like the others, with dark, curly auburn hair and shadows under his eyes. His features marked him as belonging to the royal house of Autumn, just like Gail.

They were all watching him. Waiting for him to speak.

But what could he say?

Sorry your sister is dead, and it's partly my fault?

He slid down the wall and sat on the floor, pulling his knees up and resting his forehead on them, completely drained.

'Gail, you okay? You... err... you look a mess,' William said, offering a crooked smile, signing as he spoke.

'Um... yeah. Bit of trouble with an ogre,' Gail signed back, forcing a smile but speaking aloud too keeping the mental link between them firmly closed. He could feel William pressing at the barrier, but he wasn't ready to let him in.

'Are you hurt?' Cyn asked, frowning at the blood caking his clothes and face.

'No... it's not mine,' Gail sighed, moving his hands with effort. He already knew the next question and steeled himself for it.

'Where's Willow? Is she okay?' William asked, concern deepening as his gaze swept over Gail. If it wasn't his blood, then whose?

Why wasn't Willow with them?

CHAPTER THREE

Is that why he won't open the link? Fear prickled under William's skin. 'Gail... what happened to Willow? Where is she?'

'She... she didn't make it,' Gail said quietly, rubbing his eyes. He didn't want to see the look on William's face.

'What do you mean?' William signed quickly, forgetting to speak. Panic was written all over him.

'William, calm down,' Jacen signed, placing a firm hand on William's arm. Leaf and Hyacinth watched in tense silence.

'She's gone. They shot her. By accident,' Gail signed, then closed his eyes, ending the conversation with the sharp finality of his gesture. He pulled his knees closer, buried his head in his arms, and let the hot tears fall.

The room went silent, except for the sound of Gail's quiet, broken sobs.

'No... she's the Child of Nature—they *can't* have,' William signed, angry tears sliding down his cheeks. 'Tell me you're wrong!'

Jacen held him back as William surged forward. 'William, look at him. I don't think it's a mistake,' Jacen signed gently, his own lip trembling.

William let out a choked noise and sank to his knees.

Cyn crossed the room and sat beside Gail, wrapping her arms around him. She felt his shoulders shaking beneath her touch. *This isn't like him. He's the strong one,* she thought, *the dependable one.*

Something was *very* wrong.

She didn't understand what had been said in signs, but she didn't need to. The devastation on William's face and the broken state of her cousin said it all.

'Cyn... do you know what they said?' Leaf crawled over, his voice low and uncertain.

'No. But just look at him,' she said softly, biting her lip.

Across the room, Jacen was trying to keep William from collapsing completely.

William stared numbly at Hyacinth, who now held one of Gail's hands in silent comfort. He couldn't stop the barrage of thoughts tearing through him.

His mum had been with Willow. They'd all been at Gail's house. What the hell happened?

He crawled forward and tapped Gail's shoulder gently.

'My mum... and your dad—what happened to them?' William signed.

Gail hiccupped, then signed back without lifting his head.

'Trying to get me to safety. My dad was overwhelmed... I don't know what happened to your mum.'

He dropped his head again, curling tighter into himself.

Leaf balled his fists at his sides, watching his cousin unravel. *Gail never broke. Never.*

And now he had.